I0544777

Starting Over

THE BEGINNING

MATTHEW J. METZGER

The Beginning
ISBN # 978-1-83943-924-7
©Copyright Matthew J. Metzger 2020
Cover Art by Erin Dameron-Hill ©Copyright November 2020
Interior text design by Claire Siemaszkiewicz
Pride Publishing

Published in 2020 by Pride Publishing, United Kingdom.

THE BEGINNING

Chapter One

His car was the only one left.

Aled sighed as he collapsed into the driver's seat. The rest of the car park was devoid of life, with not even the rats feeling sociable now. A lonely light flickered above the exit. When he turned the key in the ignition, the dull echo bounced off the concrete walls and punched him in the ears.

Rather than head home, Aled sat back and finally took his personal phone out of his pocket. More than twelve hours after he'd arrived at the office, he finally had a moment to scroll through his messages. A reminder about his dentist appointment next week. One advert from Sky. A voicemail from a withheld number that could definitely wait. And a flurry from his partner, waiting at home, and his best friend, waiting in St Ives.

Gabriel: Cannelloni for dinner, y/n?

Suze: GUESS WHAT!

Tom: Big news pal!!!

*Gabriel: Suze just called. I'll start packing for you too ;)
See you later xxx*

Gabriel: Cannelloni is a no btw, the meat's gone off :(

Suze: Call me! Call me call me call me call me!

Suze: Fine, be busy.

Suze: Euan's getting a baby sister!

Suze: You're going to be an uncle again!

Aled closed his eyes as a jolt of pain burst through his chest. He should be thrilled. Should call her at once. Call her bloody mad for getting pregnant again so quickly after having Euan.

But the only thing that occurred to him was that he'd missed it all.

He'd spent almost thirteen hours at work today. Eleven of them had been wasted in pointless meetings at which nothing was decided. His lunch break had been sacrificed to firefighting about a major campaign that was in danger of going belly-up. And the final hour had been spent interviewing the last candidate for the senior account manager's vacancy. Absolutely none of it had been work. Or even worthwhile.

Meanwhile, his best friend had baby news and his partner had been making dinner and packing their cases for their weekend trip to Cornwall. Life had been moving without him. While he'd been talking campaign management, they'd been *living*.

Why?

Aled dropped the phone on the passenger seat and put the car in gear. He felt—low. Flat. The weekend holiday was overdue already, but he had the glum feeling that he wouldn't feel any better when he came back on Tuesday.

What the hell was he doing it all for?

Aled had never pretended to have a job that performed some greater good. He was a marketing executive. He'd worked for the same firm since he'd left university, almost seventeen years ago. He had a fat salary and a nice company car, and he did it so he could afford a nice house in a decent area and not have to worry about money. And given that Gabriel barely made more than minimum wage and had only been working part-time since his accident last year, the household finances rested mainly on Aled.

He couldn't afford to walk away, yet as he cruised the dark streets, weaving around taxis and early evening revellers, Aled wondered if he could really afford to stay much longer.

Once upon a time, he'd enjoyed working for the firm. When he'd been a drone with a cubicle, and his best friend Suze had worked in accounting on the next floor down. When he'd been able to go to Christmas parties and leaving dos without being eyed warily from the sidelines and dealing with suck-ups at the bar. He'd gone to work with his best friend and pseudo-sister, and his days had consisted of slagging off incompetence and making bets on when the estates manager would finally snap. They'd bitched over

Skype at work, met up for a bitch in person at lunch, then again at the end of the day.

Then he'd been promoted a few times and Suze had left to get married and start a family down south, and—

Aled squeezed the steering wheel.

And he'd started to feel *flat*.

He reached out for the stereo system and brought up the speed dial, hitting Gabriel's number. It was second, preceded only by Suze's. Gabriel had mockingly told him off for it once, and Aled had retorted that it was usually dangerous to talk to Gabriel and drive at the same time. But sexy games weren't on his mind. Gabriel was only half an hour away, yet Aled had a fierce need to hear him sooner than that.

"Hello?"

"Hey. It's me. I got out of work at last."

"Finally!" Something clanged in the background. "Sorry. I'm packing snacks for the car. Did you get Suze's news?"

"Yeah."

"She was suggesting we go down tonight so you have all of Saturday to help them celebrate, and I've packed for that but you've had a long day, so—"

It would be sensible to wait until the morning, but Aled selfishly wanted as much time as possible. He could check into the hotel at any time. And Gabriel was spending the weekend with one of his other boyfriends near Bristol, who wouldn't much care when they swung by.

"You can keep me awake until Bristol," he said. "If I'm knackered by then, I'll crash on Chris' sofa."

"Okay," Gabriel said. "Are you all right? You sound—"

Aled winced.

" — kind of flat. Are you sure everything's okay?"

"Yeah. Just work. Long day."

"Need something to take your mind off it?"

Aled laughed. "I'll definitely be too tired to drive if you start that."

"I *meant* a cuddle, you sex-obsessed swine," Gabriel said loftily.

It was all bullshit and they both knew it. Gabriel fully admitted to being obsessed with sex. If not for the fact that he *could* abstain if he really had to, Aled would have thought it was an addiction. Nine times out of ten, when they fucked, it was Gabriel who started it.

But the haughty tone brought a smile to Aled's face, metaphorical sun starting to glimmer through the moody clouds in his head. Gabriel's faux-bitch attitude was funny given his usually placid nature, and it lifted Aled's spirits. Gabriel in general lifted his spirits. Somehow, he always knew the right thing to say and the right way to be.

"Are you driving?"

"Yeah."

"Could you stop at the petrol station and get a tin of those fruit sweet things for the drive down?"

"Sure." Practicalities helped a little, too. "Need to fill up anyway. I'll be home in about half an hour."

"Okay. You want a special greeting?"

"Nah. A hug will do fine. See you soon."

"Love you!"

He hung up and cruised into the petrol station in a slightly better mood. Gabriel had a sunny sort of personality. He bounced. He'd been a bit of a mess after his accident, and during the whole Michael fiasco a couple of years ago, but he'd been riding a high since he'd been allowed to ditch the last of the medication.

He'd even managed his first bike ride last month, and he'd been ridiculous ever since. And when he was buoyant, he pulled everyone else up to the surface with him, bad day at work or no bad day at work.

Yet it still felt like Aled wasn't getting to see too much of that cheerfulness lately. He'd said goodbye when Gabriel was still half-asleep in their bed. He'd not been able to so much as text. And yesterday had been the same, and the day before, *and* the day before...

He mused as he filled up the car and fetched the requested tin of sweets. The problem was, he couldn't see a feasible way out of the problem. If he jumped ship to another company, he'd run into the same issue. If he requested part-time, the company would quickly sideline him and coax him into quitting altogether so they could save money and resources for the full-time staff. He knew how it worked because he'd seen it before, and even exploited it to get rid of a couple of grossly incompetent underlings before now. And to top it off, Aled had grown too used to his lifestyle. Scaling it all back for a lesser-paying job would introduce a whole new set of problems. And who was going to hire a thirty-seven-year-old man to start a new career? It was too late for change.

Christ, was he entering a midlife crisis? He hoped not. He wasn't planning on thirty-seven being the midpoint of his life, for one.

Squaring his shoulders as he got back behind the wheel, Aled decided to talk it over with Gabriel, and with Tom and Suze over the weekend. Something had to change, and they'd probably have some good ideas. He was spending too much time at a job he was coming to hate, and he was missing out on his family as a result. To hell with that.

Home—for the moment—was a tidy little house in Newmillardam, south of Wakefield where Aled had spent most of his life. It had played home to three of them for several months last year, but Gabriel's other boyfriend had eventually gone back down south once Gabriel had healed from his car accident, and now the house was just theirs again. Aled missed the extra company a little, but not the lack of room. It *really* wasn't built for three, after all.

He pulled up outside and sat back for a minute, just looking at the warm yellow light glowing through the windows. The curtains were drawn, but a shadow moved in the kitchen. Next door's cat prowled along their front garden wall and vanished in a flurry of fur when Aled stepped out of the car.

It was home.

Their home. The first one they'd bought together. The one marked by the pair of them, rather than just him, and Gabriel slotted in around the edges. He knew if he walked in, he'd find Gabriel's uniform draped over the radiator in the hall, and their walking coats wrestling for room on the same hook. His gym kit would have been put through the wash when Gabriel got home from his half-shift that morning. There'd be something to eat waiting in the microwave for him, even if it wasn't cannelloni. The dishes would have been washed but left to dry on the rack for Aled to put away when he got back. Every room would be perfectly balanced between pristinely tidy but not clinically clean. Lived-in, but neat. Gabriel had taken over most of the chores when he'd first moved in, back in the old house, as an exchange for working fewer hours and bringing in less money. Aled had let him, and the house was far nicer for it. Tonight, Gabriel was probably packing for the drive south, but usually Aled would find him watching TV or flirting with one of his other boyfriends on his phone. Occasionally he'd already be in bed, but only if he had an early shift in the morning.

Aled stood on the path, staring at their front door, and wanted nothing more than to walk inside and never come out.

Then next door's cat shot past his ankles in pursuit of something with a very short lifespan. Aled rolled his eyes, stuck his key in the lock and let himself in.

"I'm home!"

"Kitchen!"

The sight that greeted him brought a lump to Aled's throat. Two cases set by the door, ready to go. Gabriel in the kitchen, packing digestive biscuits into a tin for the drive down. Two cans of Pepsi were sitting in a cooler bag, waiting to go in the glovebox. Two more were set out on their own for the cupholders. The sat nav was charging on the counter, and the whole kitchen was permeated with the warm smell of baking, the results presumably contained in the second tin sitting on top of the — thankfully off — glass hobs.

Home.

It all bubbled over.

"I don't think I can do this anymore," Aled whispered.

And everything ground to a halt.

Chapter Two

"I don't think I can do this anymore."

Gabriel carefully finished emptying the digestives into the tin, then closed the lid and said, "You have twenty seconds to tell me you're talking about something other than us."

Aled groaned. He looked exhausted, but a smile flickered around the edges of his mouth all the same. The half-joke had worked. He slipped off his tie, looped it around Gabriel's waist and towed him into a hug that smelled like cheap coffee and fusty air conditioning.

"I mean work." A stubbly kiss grazed Gabriel's ear. "This is fine."

"Fine?" Gabriel said, keeping up the act. "There goes your blow job on the M5."

Aled huffed a weak laugh before letting go. "Not in the mood," he admitted.

Gabriel ran his hands down Aled's arms, considering his options. If Aled wanted to get on the road, he'd rush to get out of the door. But he was plainly miserable, and Gabriel wanted to fix that first.

They could always go tomorrow. So he picked at the cufflinks, sliding cotton and silver apart until pale wrists were exposed, then lifted one and sucked on the pulse beating gently beneath the skin. It quickened.

"Tell me about it," he murmured, then scraped his teeth along the vein.

"Thirteen hours at work today, and I spent most of them in overpopulated meetings without a single thing being agreed on or done," Aled complained. "Imogen has decided…"

Gabriel untucked the dress shirt from the overpriced trousers and skimmed his thumbs around the waistband. He didn't give two shits about what Imogen had decided. Aled was unhappy, and it was Gabriel's job to make it better. And a fast, easy solution — a quick plaster over the wound to stem the bleeding — was to rile him up. Get him hard then get him off. Gabriel slid the buckle free and followed it to the floor, nuzzling the front of Aled's silk boxers before pulling them down and taking Aled's soft cock into his mouth.

Above him, Aled groaned…then kept talking.

Gabriel had mixed feelings about sucking cock. They didn't exactly taste like ice cream, and he was usually skullfucked by his preferred partners rather than given the time and space to actually suck anything, so it was unfamiliar territory. On the other hand, he had a submissive streak a mile wide, and a kinky streak a mile wider than that, and there was always a thrill to being used and pseudo-abused — so the prospect of getting Aled off and getting nothing in return was strangely appealing, even if he wasn't going to get drilled like he usually was.

He worked at the head until Aled was half-hard, then drank him in like water in large, messy gulps until he could feel the pre-cum against the back of his mouth. Half-hard became rock solid in a matter of seconds as he massaged the shaft with his tongue. A gentle hum was all it took to interrupt the flow of Aled's words, then a hand tugged on his hair.

Gabriel looked up and instantly got wet.

Aled was frowning down at him. Still in his dress shirt. Mouth a grim slash in a stern face.

Dominant.

"And to top it off," Aled said slowly, "I get home and tell my slut of a partner that I'm not in the mood for a blow job, and he thinks he can get away with one anyway?"

Gabriel opened his throat as Aled pushed. He was well-practised. Trained, even. Deepthroating came effortlessly, but he clenched his hands over his knees as the airless seconds ticked by. They didn't do breathplay. He'd let Aled block his air for a moment or two, then he'd flash him a fist. A silent safeword.

In a *moment...*

He didn't dare look away.

"When I let go," Aled whispered, "you're going to bend over the table, drop your jeans and stay silent."

Silent?

Aled let go. Gabriel gulped air for a moment, getting his bearings, before sinking back into the obedient headspace. And he *needed* to be obedient when Aled was in a mood, or it would hurt more than Gabriel was really after right before a long car journey.

Aled did offer a hand to haul Gabriel to his feet, then lent both to smash him down onto the kitchen table. Jeans were yanked down. A sharp smack was a brief punishment for the lack of underwear. The kitchen was warm, but the air on his skin felt cold.

Then Gabriel got the idea as the soap dispenser squeaked.

"Oh my God. No-no-no—"

"No isn't your safeword."

His head was ground down against the wood. Hair strained. Gabriel sucked in a lungful of air, mind racing. He wanted to obey, wanted to do whatever Aled needed to feel better, but self-preservation was kicking in, too. It had been weeks since—since—

"Yellow!"

The hand in his hair eased. The tip of Aled's cock stayed perfectly still against his arse. Yellow was the warning light. Not quite stop, not quite no, but a pause, a maybe. If Gabriel had said red, it would have ended everything. And he didn't want to end *everything*, but—

"Front," he said. "Please. It'll hurt. And not the good kind of hurt."

He didn't much like anal sex at the best of times. It didn't get him off sexually, and while being used like a filthy whore was *amazing*, why bother getting that via the back door when he could get the same feeling in the front *plus* an orgasm? And up the arse, almost dry with no preparation, before sitting in a car for several hours was asking too much.

He released the breath as Aled's cock moved to tap lightly against his vagina, cold soap tingling against the labia.

"Colour."

"Gree—*fuck*!"

A cock like steel smashed into him like it owned the place. All at once, he wasn't a person with a partner and a job and interests and hobbies. He was a *thing*. A sheath. He was there to wrap his lips—any lips—around whatever dick was nearest. Everything intelligent around his brain shut down in that first thrust. He was a sex toy, a doll, a hole built to milk a dick.

"I said *silent*."

The hand that sealed his mouth was hard. It bruised his jaw. For a split second, there were other things — blunt nails, cologne, the table — but then it all became about the cock sawing him in half. Long, powerful thrusts designed to fuck and hurt, and maybe not in that order.

And God, it hurt so *good*.

It didn't take long. Aled came in short, sharp bursts of wet heat, and pulled out as soon as it was over. A drawer was dragged open, and metal clinked. Gabriel was roughly turned over and his weak limbs bent until they were locked together under the small table, wrist to wrist and ankle to ankle.

Latex snapped.

"Now how about we try this again, instead of you trying to get out of a civilised conversation by blowing me?"

"Y-yes, si*iiir* — "

The cold, impersonal feel of rubbery fingers working their way into his drenched cunt was disgustingly hot.

"I was in meetings for near-enough twelve hours today."

"Tha-that's — oh fuck — that can't have been fu-*un*!"

There were three fingers poking around inside him. Just fumbling around in there, like they were looking for something. There was an orgasm building in the base of his dick, and Gabriel began to squirm to hurry it up.

"I was bored stupid and I'm not even doing anything meaningful with it. We help companies sell pointless products. That's it. Hardly earth-shattering."

The soap dispenser squeaked again. Gabriel swore, then fought his way back to the topic at—to the topic. His cunt was the only thing at hand, and he didn't fancy trying to talk about that too.

"S-sometimes a job's just a job."

"Yeah, well, I'm tired of pretending I give a fuck in front of my boss."

"Maybe it's time to look else—*right there!*"

Gabriel liked pressure on his orgasms. Grinding them out. Squeezing every muscle as tight as it would go. And, of course, he couldn't. Aled's hand was in the way, and so the aftershocks went straight back to the fuck-ready simmer he'd been nursing before. Aled taunted him by scraping a latex-covered thumb over his cock, dragging him through another climax within seconds of the first.

"Oh God, *please*—"

"Please what?"

"Let me come properly!"

"You're coming just fine, you fucking slut," Aled replied casually. "You just squirted on my best shirt."

"You *know* it doesn't feel the same."

"I know we're getting off topic."

Gabriel whined as that evil thumb began to work its way in to join the rest of the hand, and wrestled his brain back online. He was about to get fisted, and there was no fucking way he'd have the brain cells to carry on a conversation once Aled got his whole hand in there.

"S-so get another job. L-look elsewhere. I can always ask for more—fuck—hours at—at work i-if money is the issue."

"Could always rent you out," Aled said casually, even though they both knew it to be a lie. "Make a fortune."

He curled his hand into a fist, and drove it deeper until the dangerous edge of pain sparked along Gabriel's nerves and he felt the ticking of Aled's watch against his skin.

"But then this would be like flinging a sausage down a motorway."

"S-speaking of motorways, shouldn't we get going?"

"Too late. Your cocksucking put paid to that," Aled said. "I'm tired and it's late. Let me check."

Gabriel yowled as the hand was dragged back out—thankfully not clenched—and the glove ripped off.

"Yes," Aled said. "At least another hour before I'll be driving anywhere. I need to wake myself up a bit. So—"

Gabriel whimpered as rubber snapped, and fresher, dryer, less lubricated latex forced his lips apart again.

"—we've got all the time in the world."

The fist drove back up into him until Gabriel was sure his cunt didn't even *go* that deep, and he was fucked on it in idle thrusts to make the table shake and the ceiling swim dizzyingly above him. The climaxes followed one another like train carriages, all torturingly weak and delivering nothing like the euphoria Gabriel wanted.

"A-are you feeling better?" he begged.

"Much, thank you."

"So—so—"

"Is the slut tired?"

The harsh word scraped along Gabriel's dick, thick as fingers. It was like doing drugs. The whole room was a white abyss — and it was *hell*.

"Yes."

"Does the slut want to come properly?"

"Oh God, yes."

"My hand not good enough?"

Trap.

"Your cock is best."

Avoided. Aled chuckled, and the fist relaxed. Retreated. Gabriel sagged against the wood, gaping hollow.

"Well, there's a couple of options here, slut."

Gabriel *hated* options.

"You can give me what I wanted the first time, with a nice sharp clip on your cock to help you along —"

A wet finger slid past his cunt and tapped his arse like knocking on a door.

" — or you can get back on the floor and I can fuck the hole in your face to shut you up instead."

Anal, but the best orgasm of his life from the clip. Or a facefuck and probably nothing? It wasn't even a contest.

But —

Gabriel lifted his exhausted head and caught Aled's eye. For a split second, he shoved the game aside and spoke not as his owner's live-in sex slave but as Aled's boyfriend.

"Lube. *Properly.*"

Aled nodded once.

Gabriel dropped his head back and closed his eyes.

"You can always have what you want, sir."

Later, drifting in a sea of post-orgasmic bliss and rippling like the surface of a still pond with every table-breaking thrust, Gabriel curled his fingers around the chain keeping him prisoner to the ecstasy, and a thought drifted across his scattered mind.

It wasn't the job.

Not really.

It was Suze.

Chapter Three

It was just after midnight when he heard the car pull up outside.

Swinging his legs off the bed, Chris passed from the lacy bedroom to a barren hall, fresh paint still drying on the walls. Dust sheets covered everything, and the stench of white spirit still lingered around the kitchen archway. When he opened the front door, Noodle skirted in around his legs with a happy chirrup. Aled's expensive car gleamed at the end of the road, headlights slicing through the dark and a light mist swirling in the beams — then it took off into the night, leaving a shadow by the hedge.

That was — unexpected.

"Is everything okay?" Chris asked as the gate squeaked. "I made up the spare room if he wants to stay."

Gabriel came to the door alone, rucksack thrown over his shoulder.

"It's fine. He's just had a rotten day at work and wants to see his sister sooner rather than later," Gabriel said, and stretched up for a quick kiss. "Miss me?"

"Always."

"How you doing?" Gabriel asked as he stepped into the stripped hall.

Chris raked a hand over his bare scalp. "Okay. I think."

The shock had worn off, at least. Expecting to wake up and hear her singing in the kitchen. Be shouted at for slamming the door. The smell of her favourite potpourri had faded before he could find out what it was and replace it, but it felt like he'd only reopen the wound if he did it now.

"I guess the paperwork came through if you've started redecorating?"

"Yeah. All mine."

Mum had bought the bungalow decades ago. Chris knew every nook and cranny like he knew the back of his own hand. His grandparents had lived with them for a little while when they got too old to look after a house of their own. His earliest memories cast the shadow of his grandfather in the battered armchair in front of the TV. He'd been conceived on the kitchen table, so that had been the first to go. There were photos of him and his brother Tim learning to walk in the kitchen. Tim's ashes were scattered in the garden with their grandparents — and last week, Mum's too.

Because the bungalow was now his.

"What are you going to do with it?" Gabriel asked.

Chris swallowed. The lump in his throat had been there for weeks, but at least now it was just a scratchy irritant. The urge to cry had dulled. Life was starting to reorient itself around the void his mother had left behind.

And they hadn't even been close. He'd never really imagined he'd grieve for her, the stranger who'd been perpetually disappointed by him, but he had. There was a hole were there hadn't been one before. A silence in the little house that still felt wrong.

"Sell it," he said.

Gabriel slid an arm around his waist, and said nothing.

"Too many memories to keep it," Chris added eventually. "So…so I'm doing it up, and selling it on, and then…I don't know. Buy somewhere else with the money, I guess. I don't know."

"I get it." A hand squeezed his elbow. A kiss brushed his cheek. "You know what sounds nice? Pyjamas and a big thick duvet and falling asleep to one of your action films."

That did sound good.

"Deal."

He ducked into the kitchen to feed Noodle and make some tea while Gabriel changed. Chris was awkward around bodies. He liked to cuddle, and even kiss if there wasn't too much in the way of tongues going on, but anything else made his skin crawl. And Gabriel usually came with evidence of the anything else. Bruises and bite marks and sometimes bits of jewellery or bondage gear. So Chris made the tea, and knocked before going back into his bedroom, and was relieved to see Gabriel already in his baggy T-shirt and boxers, sitting cross-legged on the end of the bed as he fired off messages to someone from his phone.

"Aled?"

"Kevin. Almost missed my check-in. Can you plug my charger in?"

"Sure. Picked a movie?"

"Whatever's good."

Chris picked. Gabriel texted. They moved around like it was every night of his life, and Gabriel climbed into his bed — his spot, no less — and held up a corner of the duvet invitingly.

"Get in here."

"Am I big spoon or little spoon?"

"Big spoon."

"Mouthful of hair it is."

"You love it."

He did. The warmth. The soft weight in his arms. The way Gabriel wriggled into him. The breathing ribs under his elbow. The way he felt the excited squeak and the croon when Noodle jumped up and Gabriel cooed at him.

"Who's *this*?"

"Mum's cat. Noodle."

"Hello, beautiful."

Noodle purred and squashed up against Gabriel's chest for a nap. It left Chris' hand trapped between a loose breast and a rumbling cat, but with the T-shirt in the way, it didn't feel bad. He even managed a gentle squeeze, and Gabriel hummed pleasantly.

The empty hole in the house — in Chris' chest — started to close.

"Thanks for coming," Chris whispered.

"I'm just sorry I couldn't come sooner. Or to the funeral."

"It's okay. I don't think I could have coped with your beard outing me in front of my uncles."

"Dicks?"

"Yeah."

"Well, least you don't have to bother with them again."

"No," Chris agreed. "Mum left me everything. And they weren't interested in helping scatter the ashes.

Don't have to see them ever again if I don't want. So that's it. That's — I have no family left."

"It's not so bad," Gabriel said. "Some families don't deserve the distinction."

"Did it still feel weird for you, though?"

Gabriel hummed. "Well, if you told me right now my mother had died, I'd buy a pair of tap shoes and dance on the bitch's grave. She was the most awful, abusive, violent cow I've ever met. *Ever.* But — it did feel a little funny when my granddad died, so yeah. I didn't even like him much, but it still felt strange the first time I was due to go over to Pudsey and didn't."

Chris dropped both arms to lie around Gabriel's waist and squeezed. He closed his eyes to drink in the smell of him. Still as familiar as if he always lay here.

"But it's okay to dump the rest of them," Gabriel said. "I haven't seen my uncles since my granddad's funeral. Or my mother since the accident. Or my brothers and sisters since I was a teenager."

Chris winced at the mention of the hospital.

"Did she try again?"

"Nope. Haven't seen anyone in my family since you scared her at the hospital. Never did figure out how she knew I was there."

Chris smiled into the back of Gabriel's head. He'd gone up north to stay with them after Gabriel's car accident, mainly to look after him while Aled was at work. And an accidental but very happy perk had been that he was at the hospital the day that Gabriel's loathed mother had turned up to try to visit. Chris never thought of himself as a hard man, but he looked hard enough to block the way. And apparently, it had worked even better than he'd thought.

"Do you miss her?"

"My mother?" Gabriel asked. "Like fuck I do."

Chris hummed. He'd been distant from his mum, and there'd always been a sense that she was quietly ashamed of him, disappointed in him, that he'd never been as good as his brother. But she hadn't been abusive, either. She had been Mum of the Year compared to Gabriel's.

"I'm... Does it sound bad if I say I'm just glad it's over?"

Mum had had cancer. On and off for the last decade. He could hardly remember her with energy or hair. It had been a long, long slide towards the end, and she'd hated every minute of it. Eventually, she'd refused any more treatment — and it had still taken five months for the lump to take her. Chris felt her absence, missed her, mourned her...yet there was a large part of him that wished it hadn't taken so long and so much suffering.

"No," Gabriel said gently.

Chris squeezed. "She's — you know, it sounds trite, but she's at rest now."

"Yeah."

"Do you believe in an afterlife?"

"I don't know," Gabriel said. "I guess I'll find out someday. That's good enough for me."

Chris hummed. Logically, he didn't. It made no sense for there to be an afterlife. But emotionally, he wanted there to be. He wanted to think she'd found Tim again. That she had the energy to do things again. That she could exist without the pain.

But of course, she didn't exist anymore, and his emotions came circling right back to his rationality.

"It gets easier," Gabriel murmured. "The grief, I mean."

"Yeah. I know."

"But if you ever need to talk, you know where to find me."

"Thank you."

"And if you need practical advice about what to do with the house, I'm sure Aled would be happy to help. He's good at all that money stuff."

Chris chuckled. He and Gabriel both came from poverty, but Aled's mum had been a doctor and given him a significant boost up the fiscal ladder. Aled had money that Chris had never even dreamed of.

"That'll be useful," he said. "I've no idea what to do next. I don't really want to stay in Nailsea on my own, but the North's not for me, either. What do you think about maybe a halfway point?"

"What, like shift up a bit so the journey's not so long?"

"Yeah."

"Honestly, I'd hang fire," Gabriel said. He wriggled over in Chris' arms, planting his head on the pillow inches from Chris' nose. Noodle meowed, then climbed over that trim waist to settle between them instead. "Aled's miserable about his job, and Suze is pregnant again and it really got to him this time."

"So?"

"So…I might try and persuade him to move south," Gabriel said. "He's depressed so far away from his family, and you're here, so I might try and push for somewhere like Exeter. Closer to them but closer to you, too."

Chris curled his fingers around a chunk of Gabriel's T-shirt, rubbing the worn cotton between finger and thumb.

"If — if you came south, I might…"

Could he?

"Might what?" Gabriel prompted gently.

Chris took a deep breath.

"I might move too," he said. "If—if, you know, you went somewhere down in the southwest, I might—Exeter sounds nice. Or Plymouth or something."

Gabriel blinked. "Really?"

"Yeah."

"You'd come with us?"

"If you did," Chris insisted. "I mean, it's obviously—he might not go for it. He's a northerner. It might be weird down here for him. Has he actually *said* anything?"

"No," Gabriel said. "But that's just Aled for you. He ticks it over in his mind for a bit before he'll sound it out. And I think we're in the ticking stage. But he was really upset when he got home this evening, and I know he misses them like crazy. And to be honest, I think he misses you a little bit, too. Having more company around and having someone to gang up on me with."

Chris rolled his eyes, and Gabriel laughed.

"You totally did."

"And you deserved it," Chris deadpanned.

"Rude."

"The truth hurts sometimes."

Gabriel flipped him off, then cuddled into his chest. Noodle grumbled, then started to purr noisily as a reminder of his presence.

"Does Aled like cats?"

Gabriel laughed. "No idea."

"Well, he better learn."

"Don't make any solid plans yet," Gabriel said. "But I'll work on Aled and—and maybe we can all get together sooner than next summer."

Chapter Four

Someone was banging on the door.

Aled cracked open an eye and stared at the ceiling. Where—

Oh.

Hotel room. St Ives. Cornwall.

Banging on the damn door.

"Just a minute!" he shouted, and rolled out of bed.

The hotel room looked pristine. He'd arrived at almost four in the morning and had checked straight in. His bag sat in the corner, still packed. The en suite door hadn't been opened. The sheets were only disturbed on his side of the bed, the other half still perfectly tucked in and the chocolate dead centre in the middle of the unused pillow. His clothes marked a trail from door to bed, like he'd died halfway there. He hadn't even texted Tom or Suze to say he'd arrived, but no doubt someone on Reception had squealed to the owner's daughter-in-law.

Because, of course, whenever they came down to stay, they were put up for free or very cheaply in one of the many hotels across Devon and Cornwall owned by Tom's father. Aled was hardly going to say no to mate's rates on a fancy hotel, was he? And Gabriel never said no to a game in a hotel room either.

Aled would happily have said no to the incessant hammering on the door at—he checked his watch—half-past-eight, mind.

"What?" he demanded, jerking it open.

Suze just squealed and threw her arms around his neck.

"Hello!" she shrieked in his ear. "Oh my god, hello-hello-hello!"

Aled grinned and folded his arms around her, squeezing tightly.

He and Suze went way back. They'd gone to nursery school together and had been firm friends ever since. Suze had been the first person who knew he was bisexual or into BDSM, Aled the first person to know Tom wasn't just another bad idea in Suze's long history of shitty ex-boyfriends. He'd given her away at her wedding. Her son was named after his late father. They were *family*, even if Suze's ash-blonde hair definitely hadn't come from Aled's ginger family background.

In an instant, the flat depression vanished. Energy flooded in. He was *home*, home like he was home when he walked in the door and reeled Gabriel in for a kiss. Home like the cuddle chair with its soft fleece blankets. Home like home used to feel, before his promotions and her marriage and the hundreds of miles between them.

He squeezed one more time, twirled her just to make her yell at him then dropped her again.

"Get dressed," she said, plucking the waistband of his briefs with zero sense of modesty or shame. "I'm taking you out to breakfast and then you're taking me out to lunch!"

"No Euan?"

"Tom takes him to the park on Saturday mornings," she said. "We'll meet them for lunch."

Tom was from an enormous family. Suze's family were shits but thankfully estranged, so she pretended to be an only child. Aled had predicted Tom's tribe would win on how many children they'd have, and once he was dressed and had found his wallet and car keys, he prodded her flat belly and said, "Called it."

"Oh shut up." She pinked. "It wasn't on purpose."

"I didn't need to know that. How far along?"

"Only four weeks," she said. "I was feeling dizzy and weird whenever I fed Euan, so the GP took some bloods and here we are."

"Congratulations? I think?"

"Uh, *definitely!*"

"Congratulations!" Aled repeated with overexaggerated cheer. She punched him in the arm.

"We're hoping for a girl this time. Tom wants at least one of each and I'm not having more than two…"

"Uh-huh. Like you were going to wait after Euan."

Aled didn't like kids, nephews or nieces or otherwise. Suze, on the other hand, had always wanted babies. But they were the same age, so he wasn't surprised that she'd gotten pregnant again sooner rather than later. There might not be much later left.

So he let her gush about her baby son and her hopes for a daughter all the way down to the street and into a cosy little café selling gloriously fat bacon sandwiches. He didn't even tease her about the shockingly brief span between one pregnancy and the next. The short sleep after a long day had made him hungry, and he guzzled two butties before sitting back with a black coffee and watching Suze spread jam on her toast.

"I've missed this," he admitted.

"Me too. No Gabriel this time?"

"He wanted to drop in and visit Chris."

"Ahh. How's everything going?"

"With me and Gabriel? Fine." He shrugged. "Same as always. I assume things are fine with Chris. Gabriel's making noises about going abroad for a holiday this year and he's trying to talk Chris into coming with us."

"Ooh, anywhere nice?"

"Nah, he's just angling for some adventure. He's never been abroad."

"What, ever?"

"Nope."

"Wow."

"I was thinking Greece. Nice resort somewhere. They can bugger off biking and I can lie in the pool all day."

Suze laughed, propping her chin on her hand. "Well, don't book anything yet."

"Why?"

She made a face. "Tom made me promise not to tell."

Aled just waited. He liked Tom. He considered him a friend. But he was and always would be Suze's husband first and Aled's friend second. Aled was always on Suze's side, and everybody knew it.

And it worked in reverse, too. Tom had been made aware, very early in their relationship, that Aled was in effect the father-in-law. He was the other man in Suze's life who took priority over even her husband. And if Tom tried to interfere with that, he would be writing his own divorce papers.

Thankfully, Tom knew what trusting his partner looked like, and had never been particularly bothered by it. Even when Aled's marriage had fallen apart and his now ex-wife had asked one too many times if he and Suze were *really* just friends, Tom hadn't batted an eyelash. *He* knew it had never been true. And it helped that he and Aled got along on a personal level, too.

So Aled let Suze pretend to keep a secret for a few minutes, idly stirring his coffee and knowing full well it was just for show, until she huffed and waved some jammy toast at him.

"Fine, but act surprised when he talks to you."

"Okay."

"His dad is retiring."

Aled raised his eyebrows. "Uh. Good for him? Bit young, isn't he?"

"He had a cancer scare—"

"Oh God."

"No, no, he's fine—it was a harmless cyst. But it put the wind up him and Tom's mum, so he's retiring so he can enjoy more golf. And he's handing the business over to Tom."

"To Tom? Why not one of his brothers?"

Tom had a platoon of siblings, a mix of full, half and step. As far as Aled could gather, a man with a horde of children had married a woman with another horde of children and made a third horde together. Tom was one of the third horde—and not the oldest, either.

"Well, he's splitting the pubs off for Daz to look after—he's got more experience in that area anyway—but Tom's taking over the hotels and hostels part of it. Nobody else is interested in actually keeping it, and there's this huge deal about leaving anything to Paul since he got married because oh my *God*, his wife—"

Aled let her derail the conversation for a while on April, the hideously unsuitable gold-digging wife, before steering her back on track.

"Congratulations, I suppose, but what does Tom getting a big promotion at Daddy's business have to do with me?"

Suze fidgeted. "Promise to act surprised."

"I already did."

"Do it again."

"Fine, Jesus. I promise."

She nodded, then the rush of words picked up again like he'd never interrupted.

"So his dad is splitting it between them on the proviso that they don't sell up to any big chains or investors. It has to stay in the family, right? But he's not done himself any favours because he's been sort of coasting along for the last decade rather than really reinvesting or updating anything. So some of the properties are dated and others need urgent works and there's a couple Tom's going to have to sell as residential anyway because of legal requirements. So the whole chain needs updating and a new marketing strategy put in place. And the *pub* chain is doing well, but it has a lot of capital just sitting around doing nothing. And Tom and Daz both agree it's time to start *really* expanding. Push into other parts of the country, or even into Ireland and the Channel Islands, take advantage of all the ferry services —"

Aled frowned. "They have *that much* capital?"

"Oh yeah. This is all without needing a loan from the bank. If they got a business loan approved, they could go international overnight."

"Holy shit," he said. "That's insane. Why would he just bank it all?"

"I told you his dad was coasting the business along. I think he was too old to take on the projects but too young to admit he wanted to step down yet. He's kind of a control freak."

Aled grunted. "No way to run a business."

"No, but Tom's determined to revitalise it. And he can. He's been in talks with all their managers already, and he's drawn up an investment strategy, and the refit in Plymouth has already started to raise bookings. Only thing is, he's going to need to take on more staff to keep it up."

"So?" Aled said. "I don't know the first thing about running a hotel, Suze."

"No, but you know how to sell just about anything."

Aled frowned.

"He needs someone with marketing experience," Suze clarified. "He needs a campaign strategy. A campaign manager with *skill*. He needs to reach new customers *and* new investors, all over the world. And we both know you're the best. He wants *you*."

Aled stiffened, coffee halfway to his lips.

"We miss you," Suze said beseechingly. "You're too far away from your family. And you're *good*, Aled. You've raked in *millions* for Foster over the years. Tom could really do with your help. You could change everything for the business. And this could set all our lives back on track. We'd all be together again, like we're supposed to be."

Aled laughed weakly. "Tom can't afford my help. Not to cover all the perks I get now."

The company car, the private health insurance, the dental plan, the insane holiday allowance, the frequent flyer miles, the life insurance, the annual bonus...

"No," Suze admitted. "It *would* be a salary drop. But it's still good pay — especially for round here — and you'd be with your family. You'd be able to afford property with the wage Tom's going to offer you. You'd not be struggling for anything."

Aled twisted the cup in his hands, head and heart at war. He could come *home*. But he wasn't a fool. The salary would be significantly smaller. No more nice car, for one. And Tom's company wasn't likely to be picking up the tab for fuel or expenses as much as a multinational advertising agency. They might have to rely more on Gabriel's job, and he'd need to be able to find one down here. Would Gabriel even agree to come? He had his own life up north — Kevin and Judith being top of the tree — and even outside of his long-term relationships, he still occasionally used dating apps to find a willing stranger from time to time and enjoy some seedy hotel room sex with someone he'd never see again. Would Gabriel —

Aled's heart twisted.

He wanted to say yes. To call Tom right this minute and say yes. He'd be close to his family, and the possibility was the most tempting offer Aled had had in years.

But what if he had to leave Gabriel behind to get it?

Chapter Five

There was a hand on the back of his neck.

Gabriel gasped at the sudden stab of pain, and the hand clamped over his mouth instead. He clenched, but it was no use — the hard cock drove into him anyway. The grunt in his ear was animalistic. The smack of balls against his arse was obscene. The second thrust was just as hard. And the third. One after another. Bang, bang, bang. Just a warm body to wank into.

And wet.

Gabriel shoved a hand between himself and the sheets, and started rubbing one out. Nobody else was going to do it. He was there to collect cum and make others feel good. Which right now meant shutting the fuck up and staying still until it was done.

Fuckmeat doesn't get better than this.

Gabriel loved waking up mid-fuck. Being used was one of his major kinks. He *loved* it, even when he didn't get off. Almost all his kinks boiled down, ultimately, to being used like a sex doll. Like a toy. Like sex was his purpose, and if he didn't like it, too bad.

But the force behind it made all the difference. The hand gagging him. Having his arm pulled out and twisted up behind his back because he was moving too much. The force of a dry fuck with no preparation. The hot, wet flood when Chris came, and the hard smack on his arse before he was abandoned in the middle of a cold, lonely bed with hot cum leaking out of him. Sleazy. Dirty. Grim.

Amazing.

The shower came on in the bathroom, and Gabriel turned over to spread his legs, finger the cum back out of himself, and jack off in the mess. Fuuuuck, that felt good.

Being used was more or less the kink that underpinned every other one he had — but sadly Chris never played games. He fucked — and not often, at that — then it was over. And it left Gabriel with an insatiable itch and nobody around to scratch it.

So before the last shocks had even died away, he texted Aled.

Me: I need a filthy dirty game. Can we play when you get here?

To his surprise, Aled was already up.

Aled: Just been fucked, have you?

Me: Yep x

Aled: Let me guess…

Aled: He held you down and jacked off inside you, and now you want someone to really abuse you, not just use you.

Aled: You want someone to call you a pathetic slut, to leave bruises, to fuck you until you're bleeding, to make you cry, to film you degrading yourself for the sake of getting off.

Aled: Am I close?

Gabriel let out a long, shuddering breath.

Me: Not fucking close enough WHEN YOU'RE IN CORNWALL, YOU ARSE.

Aled: That's no way to talk to your betters.

Me: What you going to do, punish me?

There was a long pause. The shower shut off in the bathroom. Gabriel fidgeted on the bed, hoping Chris would stay out for a little longer, just in case Aled gave him something to work with. Sometimes, Aled just laughed at his indignation. And sometimes, he'd give Kevin's sadism a run for its money. Gabriel wasn't sure he wanted it *that* violent, but he wanted *something*.

Aled: See how I feel. There's a toy in your bag if you want it though.

Gabriel crawled to the end of the bed, hoping for a ribbed dildo or his bullet vibrator, and expecting a chastity belt. Chastity belts were like an insult to his sex drive — and a cattle prod to his submission. He hated them and loved them in equal measure. And Aled had an insulting sense of humour sometimes.
"Holy fuck."
The door opened.
"Do you want break — what the fuck is that?"

Gabriel laughed, turning Aled's present over in his hands. It was rather obvious what it was. A massive dildo, complete with balls and a proper fucking function. It was an absolute monster, and originally a Christmas present from Kevin. He'd only used it once or twice, and its size and vibration were a fast ticket to subspace.

"It's a sex toy."

"Thanks for that." Chris pulled a face. "I'll, um. Leave you to it. Sorry."

"Sorry?" Gabriel caught his wrist. "Don't be. I like waking up like that. It just—you know, I get my own itch afterwards and I asked Aled if he'd be in the mood to abuse me later and he said he'd packed a toy."

"That's not a toy. It's a weapon. How does it even fit?"

"With difficulty. That's why it's one of the abuse toys. It hurts like hell and it's *so* good."

He climbed off the bed and skirted around to the bathroom, still in his T-shirt and nothing else. Why bother putting boxers back on? He had every intention of putting this monster to use and paralysing his brain for a while longer.

To his surprise, Chris followed.

"So…what do you do with it?"

"Depends how far you want to go," Gabriel said. "Once it's fully seated, these two rabbit ears jack you off while it vibrates. And if you attach it to a solid surface, it has a pump action so it can fuck you. You can even put water—or whatever—in the balls and if you squeeze it right when it's in you, it'll come."

Chris blinked. "Does it stop after?"

"Stop what?"

"Fucking."

"Nope!" Gabriel said gleefully.

"No wonder you like it," Chris said, leaning in the doorway as Gabriel washed the toy. "You, uh. You want to borrow one of the kitchen chairs? I have to finish painting the hall today, so…"

Gabriel's heart picked up a few paces. Get fucked in the kitchen while Chris worked in the next room?

"Please. Do you — can I — "

How the hell did he even ask? He'd never expected this. Not at Chris' house. Not in Chris' company. Chris barely slept with him vanilla-style, never mind whipped out toys and watched from the next room. The one and only time they'd *played*, Aled had somehow bewitched Chris into joining in and they'd brutally spit-roasted Gabriel between them.

Was Aled working some kind of voodoo all the way from St Ives?

"Water?" he croaked eventually around a dry mouth and clumsy tongue.

"Tiled floor."

Gabriel's mouth went dry, and the dildo slipped easily from his grip when Chris took it and turned it over to examine the balls. He unfolded the little rubber tube from between them as nonchalantly as if he were checking a car engine.

"You fill it up through this tube?"

"Yeah."

"Huh."

He walked off with it. Gabriel gawped. Chris never played. He didn't do toys. The nearest he'd got to playing was when Gabriel had once sent him a text bitching about Aled's chastity belt fetish, and Chris had forwarded it to the man himself. That was it. He didn't even like *handling* Gabriel's toys.

Was he seriously about to do this?

Gabriel trailed into the kitchen after him, staring as Chris suctioned the base to a hard kitchen chair. The cock—an obscene python of a dick that was more like being fucked with a forearm—jutted up from the wood. Dry. Bulging balls. Chris tied off the tube and stood back.

"All yours," he said.

Then he walked out. Gabriel sighed, a little disappointed, but then shook himself. It was already way more than he'd expected. He should be grateful.

He was grateful for the fuck, at least. His cunt was still a little loose, and he got the first three inches in before the girth started to hurt. Inch by inch, he fought his way down until he could finally cup the swollen testicles between his thighs. There, he paused. Tipped his head back to simply breathe. Fuck, he felt so damn full. If he breathed too deep, he swore he could feel the bastard thing pressing against all his organs. Everything ached—including his swollen cock, caught between the rabbit ears.

"Hold up."

Chris' toolkit banged on the table. Something tore. Gabriel yelped as he was blindfolded with tape. First one ankle then the other was tied to a chair leg. Then his arms to the back. Then his waist, loose enough to ride but tight enough to prevent him lifting off the cock tearing him open. Two strips over each breast, like a vest holding him into a rollercoaster, but pinching his bare nipples between the edges. In a matter of moments, he was trapped—and the toy wasn't dry anymore.

Then Chris put his boot on the rim of the chair between Gabriel's knees, and pushed.

With a deafening squeal, Gabriel was shoved away from the table until his chair hit the sink. He could sense Chris fiddling around rather than hear him. Under the arousal flooding his senses — he was about to get brutally fucked while strapped down so he could barely move, and *his asexual, sex-shy boyfriend had put him there* — Gabriel managed to conjure up a few scattered questions.

"W-what are you doing?"

"Setting up a drain."

"What?"

"There." Something sloshed. "There's about four pints of water that's going to drain into that toy. You're going to milk the lot."

"Oh holy fuck," Gabriel breathed. His cock pulsed violently. "Fuck-fuck-fuck—"

"Or I'll tell Aled you've been misbehaving."

Then he switched it on.

And Gabriel came.

He was so turned on by Chris' display of sadism that one thrust was all it took. And he was fucked through it. And the ears kept rubbing, and the tape hurt his wrists, and he couldn't see, and—

It took two climaxes before he scraped together enough sense to start fucking it back. Then the filthy rush of it fucking water out of him scattered his senses and — and —

Time slid away.

The floor was wet under his feet.

Chris calling him loud and taping his mouth shut. Gabriel had a feeling that came later, but he wasn't sure. He wasn't—

The bulging balls shuddering between his thighs.

Water.

A tide of orgasms, one after another until he cried.

Time — *sliiiiiding...*

Darkness.

Voices.

The strips coming away from his face.

Aled's smile. Aled's cock in his mouth. Aled's cum sliding down his throat as more water flushed out his cunt.

Emptiness.

Aled's car. Darkness. The radio on low. The quiet hum of the engine. A clicking indicator. Tape-sore skin, freed. Fluffy pyjama bottoms and a dressing gown. Warmth. Safety.

An afterglow like the surface of the fucking *sun.*

"What — what happened?" Gabriel croaked.

"You spent about half the day spaced out," Aled said. "How you feeling?"

Tired, sore, blissful —

"Amazing."

Aled chuckled. His hand was warm where it squeezed Gabriel's wrist.

"You were so out of it, Chris filmed you and sent it to me asking if he should be worried."

Gabriel giggled like a drunk, curling up even smaller in the dressing gown. It wasn't his, and hung far too big on him. The extra layers were comforting. The best aftercare involved cuddles, but this was a very nice, and very close, second option.

"He should be worried if he doesn't do it again," he mumbled sleepily.

Aled chuckled.

"Go back to sleep," he said. "We just reached Birmingham. Plenty of time to go."

"Mm. Did you fuck my mouth?"

"Yep."

"Was I good?"

"Nope. Total mess. Looked bloody gorgeous, though. That thing fucked you six ways to Sunday."

No kidding.

"Did I get all the water?"

"Nope."

He — and the gaping exhaustion inside him — cringed.

"When we get home, you can practice your new milking technique on my cock instead of a toy," Aled said. "So get some rest, because that's happening whether you're tired or not. And I won't be tying you up so some chair will help you out."

Gabriel groaned in relief. Thank God. Tired or not, at least Aled wasn't hung like a machine. And —

"But it'll be your arse."

Oh, fuck.

Chapter Six

Chris had to mop the kitchen floor once Gabriel left.

Truth be told, he was a little bit proud of himself. Six months ago, there was no way he would have played with Gabriel like that. Even the idea of getting so sexually involved — even though he had barely touched him — had been abhorrent and made his stomach turn. A year ago, he'd come out in a sweat just *trying* to have sex with him. Vanilla sex, at that. No toys, no torture, nothing like that.

But that had been —

Fun, Chris decided. It had been fun. For the first time, he could see why Aled liked tormenting Gabriel.

He cleaned up and finished the painting before tidying that away too and heading out into the front garden to start on mending the squeaky gate. It was already dark, but the light from the front windows gave him enough to work with. And the easy job gave his mind something to do.

Like think about Gabriel's suggestion.

Ultimately, Chris didn't want to keep the bungalow. There were too many ghosts, too many reminders of growing up awkward, ashamed of himself and never quite fitting. He didn't feel like that with Aled and Gabriel. For the first time, he felt comfortable in what he was, and accepted for who he was. If they judged him at all, it was a friendly sort of banter that didn't sting like his mum's quiet watchfulness or Tim's barbed jokes. He wanted to feel like that all the time, not haunted by the questioning glances from the past.

He wasn't keen on sex. He'd never seen someone he wanted to sleep with. So what?

Finally, the *so what* felt genuine.

And while Gabriel's suggestion of moving somewhere with him and Aled had initially been terrifying — was he meant to move *in*, would Aled be up for that, what if they fought or fell apart or fell out of love — Chris' brain started to turn the scenario around as he replaced the rusty hinges. It wasn't just about moving nearer to them.

It was also a suggestion of moving away from Nailsea.

Living elsewhere, in itself, wasn't remotely odd. Chris had lived for short spells all over the place — a bedsit in Bristol, a flatshare in Portishead, the rented room in Weston-Super-Mare that he'd hated, countless army bases while he'd been serving — but the gravity of family and familiarity had always brought him back here. It was the only place he had if there was a gap between living arrangements. It was where he'd been dumped when he'd dropped out of the army in the wake of Tim's death. It was the safety net he'd relied on once Gabriel — thankfully inevitably — recovered and he wasn't needed up north anymore.

But Nailsea had never felt *good* for him.

He would always be Karen's odd young'un. Tim's shadow. He'd always be that awkward kid from school who never had a girlfriend, who was too quiet, who was up to something, who was a bit funny, like. He'd been bullied for being gay even when he wasn't, and he knew there'd been gossip the first time he'd been seen with Gabriel, who was *obviously* gay. Mum had called. Worrying. Fretting. What wasn't he telling her?

'People are talking.'

Somewhere this small, people were always talking. And Chris had a long history to talk about. From the father who'd never existed to the potential of being the only gay in a sometimes not-entirely-quietly homophobic village, there'd always been something to earn him funny looks. And in Nailsea, he was never going to get away from it. It would never be forgotten.

Somewhere else, he could shed all that baggage.

He wasn't sure he was up for living in the same house as Aled and Gabriel again—not unless it was a much bigger house—but somewhere else, near them. He'd have an instant social circle when he wanted to hang out with people. He and Gabriel had a lot in common, but he'd learned after Gabriel's accident that he got along surprisingly well with Aled, too. And Aled came part and parcel with some friends in St Ives that he'd heard good things about. He could build a new life quickly if it was near them.

A new life where he started out as Gabriel's boyfriend and Aled's mate. Where the gossip would revolve around that relationship, and not all the history that had come before it. Where his hard looks could well fit to a hard personality, not the shy, stuttering, awkward little boy who'd trailed around in Tim's long, long shadow.

Sitting back on his heels, bottom hinge complete, Chris glanced up the lane and watched curtains twitch as nosy pensioners with chronic insomnia spied on Karen Wheeler's strange son. *'He'll end up in the papers one day,'* they used to tell each other. *'He'll do something silly.'*

Chris had never figured out if the silly was supposed to be a murder or a suicide.

There'd be none of that in Newquay.

He headed back inside, filled up Noodle's dish to entice him into the house then locked up and stopped in the kitchen to heat up some leftover vegetarian chilli. His thoughts ran in circles as well as the bowl in the microwave, and he took it to bed so he could do some work on his laptop rather than eating in the still-damp kitchen. Work like job hunting. Work like flatshare prices. Work like average rents.

If he went to Devon or Cornwall, he'd need to find a new job—but here, the army and Chris' own lack of ambition helped. Aled would be thinking about prestige and promotions, but Chris was happy stacking shelves on minimum wage. He just needed to pay his bills. That was all. Everything else could come later.

So he went hunting for garages that might need apprentices, for supermarkets with a lack of till monkeys, for winter work in sorting offices to counteract the summer tourism season. He could work all summer selling ice creams to kids, then shut himself away in post rooms all winter separating Christmas presents into the correct piles. Work was work was work.

Because, outside of it, he could go biking with Gabriel *every* weekend, and without expensive train tickets to get there. He could cuddle up in bed more often, and turn the heating down a bit to counteract Gabriel's radiator of a body. Two-for-one cinema tickets beckoned.

Gabriel had hinted they'd not be apart for too long once Chris had packed up and come home again after his stint as a nurse up north, but Chris hadn't really taken him all that seriously. It had been wishful thinking at the time. Separating Aled from Yorkshire was like Somerset without the cider. It didn't work. It wasn't going to happen. Not *really*.

But now —

He remembered the way Aled had screeched away at midnight, desperate to get to St Ives to see his sister and unwilling to stop for as much as a drink, a snack and a brief hello. Unwilling to add half an hour to his journey. Unwilling to lose a minute more.

Now, Chris could see a real possibility in front of him.

* * * *

On Tuesday afternoon, he called Gabriel on the way to work.

Chris worked at a garage, but not actually fixing any of the cars. He dealt with the customers. Answered the phone. Took payments. Booked appointments. All that shit stuff. It was run by a former flatmate's brother, who hated people even more than Chris had, and had instantly offered him money to take that particular aspect of the garage off his hands. It sucked, but it was slightly more than the minimum wage, and Ryan wasn't a prick like Chris' last boss. And it was a short, pleasant walk from Nailsea into Backwell, under the railway bridge and around the corner.

So he called Gabriel as he shut the front door of Mum's bungalow, and had a cheery hello before he'd opened the repaired gate.

"So I was thinking about your whole moving plot," he said.

"That was fast," Gabriel replied.

"How — how confident are you that Aled's going to be up for it?"

"Pretty sure," Gabriel said. "But you know Aled. You have to wait for him to come to his own conclusions. Telling him what they are in advance gets you absolutely nowhere."

Chris hummed.

"Why?"

"I like the idea," Chris admitted. "I think — I think I'm going to sell up and leave Nailsea anyway. Eventually. But, um. I'll wait. Until you know where you're going to go. And then maybe I could get somewhere nearby."

He didn't hold out any hope of being able to buy outright and live without any rent or mortgage like he could in Mum's house, but that was nothing new. He'd been house-sharing right up until her illness had progressed to the final stages, when he'd moved back in to look after her in the last days. He didn't mind company. It was better than the aching silence of an empty house. And renting in Exeter or St Ives or Falmouth or somewhere down in that corner of the world wasn't going to be much different from renting in Bristol.

Hell, it would probably be a damn sight cheaper.

"That sounds perfect," Gabriel said. "I miss having you here."

"Miss you too," he mumbled as he passed a bus stop. A couple of the waiting would-be passengers, faces he'd known from infancy, eyed him curiously.

"I'll not say anything outright, but I'll push the odd button and see what response I get," Gabriel said. "To be honest, he was miserable again this morning about getting up and going to work, so I don't think the realisation is much further away."

"No rush," Chris said. "I mean, you know. I have a job and I need to finish redecorating and everything."

"Oh, *I'm* in a rush," Gabriel groused. "You try living with him when he's this antsy."

"I did. You were in hospital. It was awful."

"Oh, give over..."

Chris snorted. "Fine. Be wrong."

Gabriel tried to take back the moving idea, but Chris ignored him.

"So you reckon it's only...what? A couple of months?"

"Try a few days. Suze texted me while we were heading back. Apparently — and I never told you this — but apparently her husband Tom has offered Aled a job and his no was extremely unconvincing. She wants me to add some pressure too."

"So I take it that job means moving to...where do they live, again?"

"St Ives."

"Yeah."

"I don't know about St Ives *especially*, but it'll mean going to Cornwall, yeah. She seemed to think he was worried about what I'd think, so I'm going to drop some hints about how nice Cornwall is and see what happens."

Chris smirked. "You're ne — nefa — evil."

"Yeah, well, he knew what he was getting when he signed up."

"How?"

"It was on my Grindr profile."

"Ah."

"We weren't classy with cycling dates, you know."

Chris' face heated, though he wasn't sure if it was being called classy or the d-word.

"So I will drop lots of hints, poke the issue a little bit, see what I get," Gabriel said. "And I reckon by the end of the month, I'll get an answer. And if I'm the only thing standing in his way, then we're good to go."

"And if you're not?"

Because, after all, Yorkshire was Aled's home. Chris had felt so alien and out of place in the north that it ached, deep down inside. What if Aled felt the same way about the south?

"Then we work on your original idea," Gabriel said. "If we can't get together all the way down there with his family, then let's at least meet halfway."

Halfway sounded good.

But all the way sounded even better.

Chris crossed his fingers and hoped Aled's attachment to his family was stronger than his attachment to his home.

Chapter Seven

The weekend away was a hard reboot—and the following Tuesday at work was savage. Stupid emails, ringing phones, *meetings*, the mess of a calendar nobody had been taking care of. It almost hurt, to the point where Aled's boss, chortling, decided he'd clearly drunk too much on his jollies and sent him home by lunchtime.

'No point working with a hangover like that, eh?' he'd said.

Aled very rarely drank, and hadn't got *drunk* in years, but he played along and left anyway. Why not enjoy a bit more leisure time if it was offered free of charge? So he went home, threw a few rounds of dirty clothes into the wash, cleaned out the fridge and started to make up some meals for the coming week.

By the time Gabriel came home from the gym at six, Aled was up to his wrists in pizza dough, and a pot of homemade chilli was simmering on the stove as the third round of laundry spun in the washing machine.

Gabriel threw his sports bag down in the hall and leaned up against the kitchen doorframe, frowning.

"What's going on?" he asked suspiciously.

"I'm cooking," Aled replied.

"I can see that. Why?"

Aled pulled a face, though he couldn't deny that the suspicion was fairly well-justified. He'd always used food as a bribe, from the first time Gabriel had come over right through to, well, today.

Still, it was worth a shot at innocence.

"I can't be nice?"

A smirk danced across Gabriel's face. Aled fought to keep his own impassive.

"I'm just saying, you usually cook *after* a rough game, not before," Gabriel pointed out.

"No games," Aled said, and took a deep breath. Now. Now was the time to do it. "We need to make a decision, and not anywhere near a game."

They'd been together almost five years, and after all that time, Gabriel didn't bat an eyelash. For which Aled was immensely grateful.

"Okay," he said. "Let me get a shower first, though. The roads were *filthy*."

Aled collected the abandoned cycling gear. Once the washing machine was done, he swapped the clean laundry out and the revolting clothes in while Gabriel banged about upstairs. Next door's cat slunk in through the cat flap left in by the previous owner, hiding from the rain. Aled decided to be generous and put down a tin of tuna for the soggy beast. Rico rubbed around Aled's ankles, chirping noisily, then shoved his face into the tin before it was even set down.

"Fat git," Aled said.

Gabriel came down in his tartan pyjamas after a little while, just as Aled put the pizzas in the oven. He cosied up for a brief hug, smelling of mint and tea tree oil, then made a bid for the Coke cans in the fridge.

"Do we need the rulebook for your little chinwag?" he asked.

"Nope. It's not about that."

Gabriel cracked a can open. "Would it be something to do with Cornwall?"

Aled nodded, totally unsurprised. Suze had probably already tried to get Gabriel on board. She was sneaky like that. Hell, he wouldn't be completely surprised if Gabriel had known about the job offer before Aled had.

"Have you made a decision, or are we making one together?"

"Together," Aled said.

"Okay," Gabriel replied. "I'm all ears. After something to eat, because otherwise my stomach will do all the talking."

He put off the talk until the pizza was served and the chilli boxed up for tomorrow's lunch. They talked instead about the new gym manager — Gabriel had fucked him years ago after matching on Grindr, but the manager clearly didn't remember — and Rico sat hopefully under Gabriel's chair, even though Gabriel wouldn't share food if he were paid. Or beaten.

"So come on then," Gabriel urged, once he'd inhaled a slice of pizza. "What's this big discussion relating to Cornwall?"

Aled went for the jugular and just blurted it out.

"Tom's offered me a job."

Gabriel didn't so much as blink. "I know."

"And?"

"Do you want it?"

Aled blew out his cheeks. There was a loaded question.

"I—don't *not* want it…"

"How about you just tell me what's on your mind, all in one go, and then we'll unravel it together?" Gabriel suggested.

"All right. I want to take it. I want to be nearer to Suze, especially now she has a family. I can't stand my current job anymore. Hell, you know how I feel about *that*. But—" He gestured helplessly at Gabriel. "You're here, and I just can't walk away from you. It's not possible. Not for anything. And you belong here with Kevin and Judith. And Greg, I suppose."

Gabriel smirked at the mention of his fuckbuddy. Aled had never warmed to the obnoxiously dumb Greg, even if he did begrudgingly admit that the great lummox was harmless enough. He just couldn't see what Gabriel saw in a steroid-guzzling, overexcited puppy of a man who liked teeny-bopper music. Seeing the back of Greg would be a bonus, in Aled's opinion— but, of course, it wasn't Aled who fucked the guy.

"Not to mention it's a significant drop in pay. Nothing we can't live on, but—you know. Ford Focus instead of a company Audi. I haven't looked into house prices down there, but it's bound to be more expensive than here. It would be a step down. It wouldn't be the luxury you're used to now."

"But it *would* cover the essentials?"

"Yeah."

"So really, that's not much of a factor. I've lived on the streets," Gabriel pointed out. "As long as we could pay the essentials, then we're doing a lot better than I have been before. And you're the one with the thing for nice cars. I don't really give a shit about that. An old banger suits us fine."

Aled heaved a sigh of relief that he was sticking with *we* instead of *you*.

"The pay's not *critical*, no," Aled agreed. "But you are."

That was what it came down to. Choosing between his partner and his family.

And it was the one decision Aled just could not make. He was miserable without Suze. He hated being so far away from birthday drinks, bitching sessions over coffee, swimming classes together. He even hated missing out on Euan's milestones, and Aled didn't even *like* children. Now Nan had passed away, Suze was the only family Aled had, and he *missed* her. Missed her so much it ached.

But to leave Gabriel was unthinkable. It would be like ripping off a limb. It wasn't going to happen — he *knew* it wasn't going to happen — but if Gabriel didn't want to go, then what? How could Aled find a compromise if Gabriel wanted to stay?

Gabriel sat back with a sigh. "I have a confession to make."

Aled raised his eyebrows.

"I thought this was coming ever since Suze had the baby."

"You did?"

Euan was a few months old already, and Tom hadn't been making any noises about jobs then. Aled wondered if he really was that transparent.

"Yeah," Gabriel said. "You've been lonely since they got married, but ever since Suze said she was pregnant — with Euan, that is — you've been restless, too. Like you want to get up and go, right now. I said to Chris before he left that we'd probably be moving south ourselves before too long."

Aled snatched at the pronoun.

"We."

Gabriel smiled. "Duh."

All the muscles in Aled's spine relaxed. "You'd — you'd be okay with moving?"

Gabriel held up a finger. "Under one condition. Well, two."

"Shoot."

"You let me meet any of Kevin's conditions."

"Deal," Aled said instantly.

Kevin was the only person in Gabriel's life who was allowed to impose iron-clad rules on him outside of a sex game. He was an absolute giant of a man with a busy trade in sadism, but whom they both completely trusted. He was family — easy-going and affable with Aled, and whatever Gabriel needed at the time. Aled liked to think they got on well enough that Kevin's conditions wouldn't be unreasonable. He already had one, in that Gabriel had to be in touch at least once in every twenty-four-hour period, and Aled had always adjusted their long games to allow for that. He imagined Kevin might add a timetable for regular visits, but so what? Aled could roll with that. He'd drive Gabriel up himself if that was what it took.

"And I want Chris to come with us."

Aled hesitated.

"I miss him," Gabriel said. "I liked him being here all the time, and I miss him now. He doesn't have to live with us, like in the same house, but I want him close by. Down the road or next door or something."

"I could go along with that," Aled said. "I like him fine. But he's just a mate to me, so...you know. Maybe not the same *house*."

"Yeah, I get it," Gabriel replied. "And I'm okay with nearby. Just...you know, *near*. I'm not moving all the way away from Kevin to *still* have to sit on the train for hours to see Chris. I want to be with him. He's not just another boyfriend anymore."

"That...seems fair," Aled said. "Have you talked about it with him?"

"Yeah. The theory, anyway. But we didn't make firm plans. I wanted you to come to your own conclusions first."

"And Kevin?"

"No."

"You think he'll be okay?"

"Yeah. We've never been *in* love the way you and I are, or me and Chris are—and anyway, he doesn't feel about anyone the way he feels about Judith."

"He still loves you."

"He does," Gabriel said. "And I love him. But it's different."

Aled didn't understand it, but then he'd never had to. He simply stroked Gabriel's hand, turning it over to briefly tickle the palm.

"I don't want you to lose Kevin," he said.

Kevin was Gabriel's other regular Dominant. It had been something Aled had been presented with from the start. Gabriel was polyamorous, and while most of his other screws were either one-night stands or fuckbuddies, Kevin was different. There was a real emotional attachment to Kevin, one that Aled would not survive tangling with. If he couldn't accept Kevin, then this budding relationship with Gabriel was going nowhere.

Thankfully, Aled didn't much care about other Dominants on the scene, and Kevin was very easy to like. And Kevin's standards started and ended with how other men treated Gabriel. So Aled had passed muster early on, and they'd rubbed along just fine over the years.

"I won't lose him. He'd never let me, for one. I'll still visit all the time. And he can bring the family down to Cornwall on holidays!" Gabriel added brightly.

Aled turned the hand back over and squeezed it.

"You think *you'll* be okay?"

And there was his real worry. He'd hoped Gabriel would agree to a move — though he'd not expected it to be this easy — but it meant moving away from Kevin. The safety net. Kevin who'd steered Gabriel back to a *life* after a chaotic mess of homelessness, familial rejection and a crutch of alcoholism against depression and dysphoria. And though Gabriel had been well on the mend before Aled came along, he hadn't quite been *fine* either. There'd been too much willingness to let partners take advantage of him, too-thin defences against fear and anxiety that had crumbled when he'd lost his job.

He was much better now — and his standards for his hookups had thankfully soared — but Aled couldn't claim all the credit. A lot of it was down to Kevin. And without Kevin…

But Gabriel rubbed his thumb over Aled's knuckles and smiled.

"I think I will be," he said. "Maybe a couple of years ago, it wouldn't have been a good idea. But now? Yeah. I don't— Don't get me wrong, I love Kevin and I always will, but…I *needed* him once. I wouldn't have made it without him once. I wasn't strong enough to conquer some of those demons on my own."

"But you are now."

"Yeah. Now, I want him. I'll always want him. He and Judith and the kids will always be my family, and I'll always want them in my life. You've no chance of getting rid of them even if you wanted to. But…I don't *need* them these days. Not like I did once."

Aled squeezed tightly.

"And if I wobble—" Gabriel squeezed back. "I've got you. And Chris. And Kevin is just a train ride away. I'll be okay. You'll all make sure of it."

Aled nodded.

"So…we're moving?" Gabriel asked.

Aled let out a strangled laugh. Moving. Leaving Yorkshire. He'd never lived anywhere else.

Yet—

It felt like he'd be going home.

Chapter Eight

The very next morning, Gabriel threw down the dust sheets and started scrubbing the walls.

They'd bought a fixer-upper because the price was better, then Gabriel's accident had come just at the end of the necessaries like the gutters and the new boiler being taken care of. The result was that they hadn't got around to redecorating yet. And if they were going to sell up after all, a fresh coat of plain paint would brighten the place up in plenty of time for valuations and prospective buyers. All those property development programmes he'd watched when he'd been bedridden were finally going to pay off.

In any case, Gabriel had discovered he had a house-proud streak once they'd bought the place. It was the first private property he'd ever had his name on. The old house had been *Aled's*, both legally and emotionally. It has been his name on the deed and his ex-wife's design choices in the kitchen. It hadn't really been Gabriel's as well. And everything before it had been renting, on the social or a squat.

But this one was *theirs*. Both their names were on the title deed, and although he hadn't paid a penny towards the mortgage, he paid all the utilities. He'd picked out all the curtains, and the sofa suite had been a compromise between them instead of just what Aled had liked years before they'd met. It was partly his house, not just his home. And he'd thrown himself into learning how to look after it, and always insisted on it looking clean and tidy in a way he hadn't been bothered about before.

So, rather ironically, the living room looked like a bomb site by the time he went to work.

He didn't say anything to anyone at work — nor Aled when he popped in for a swim — but when Aled lingered until the end of the shift, Gabriel insisted on going to B&Q rather than straight home, determined to get the job finished so he could tidy up again.

"What on earth do you need to go to B&Q for?" Aled asked as he hooked Gabriel's bike up to the back of the car.

"Paint!"

"Why do you want paint?"

"I don't know, to *paint* things?"

Aled gave him a clip round the ear for that. Gabriel cackled as he ducked into the passenger seat.

"Did you tell your boss you're leaving?" Aled asked as he started the engine.

"Not yet," Gabriel replied. "I don't think I'm going to say anything until we have a moving date, to be honest. It'll just be harder to get out of the leaving party."

"Why don't you want a leaving party?"

"Booze."

Gabriel was an alcoholic. He'd run away from home in his teens, and alcohol had kept him warm on the streets — both physically and mentally. It had snowballed into a full-blown addiction before he was even twenty years old, and even though he'd been dry for years now, he wasn't stupid enough to think it was over. It was never going to be over. And he'd not have been able to rebuild his life with that crutch under his arm. So a boozy leaving do? No fucking chance.

"Ahh." Aled nodded. "Fair enough. Were you serious about the shop?"

"Um, yes?"

"Whatever you're doing, I hope you don't expect any help after the day I've had..."

Aled got the idea at B&Q itself, raising his eyebrows at the two massive cans of jasmine white that Gabriel took down from the shelf and asking if he was going to do the whole house before getting out his credit card. But when they got home, he stood aside as Gabriel lined up the rollers, and offered to make dinner.

"Please," Gabriel said.

"Want a hand with this lot, or — "

"Nope!"

Gabriel liked DIY. He'd never had a dad to teach him, and his fading memories of the shitty flats he'd been dragged up in around South London said loud and clear that his mother had never so much as cleaned the filthy pits in her life. So when he'd escaped, learning to do better had been at the top of his list. His first boyfriend had taught him how to keep a place clean, then Kevin had come along and taught him how to fix things. He'd never got the hang of electrics, but he could fix a leaky sink, bleed a radiator, top up a boiler and paint a wall with no problem.

And he enjoyed it. It was his little proof, when his mood was low and the booze aisle was terrifyingly tempting, that he'd dragged himself out of that shitty start in his life. Whenever the dark thoughts in the back of his mind rose up and asked who he thought he was, why he thought a fuck-up like him from a sink estate in shitsville could amount to anything, what made him better than a free whore, he could look at the perfectly tiled bathroom floor or the lavender bushes in the back garden and squash all the bad thoughts down again.

After all, here he was. Painting the hall of a house he part-owned while his partner made enchiladas.

"Did you check the post this morning?" Aled called, breaking Gabriel's train of thought.

"No. Got distracted by prepping the walls. Left it all on the table for you."

"There's an NHS letter for you."

"What's it say?"

Paper ripped. Aled mumbled to himself briefly, then said, "You're due a smear test."

"Urgh," Gabriel said. "Though that reminds me. What's your savings like?"

"Decent," Aled said. "Why?"

"Been thinking of having my ovaries out."

"An oophorectomy?"

"A *what*?"

"That's what it's called."

"Why on *earth* do you know that?" Gabriel demanded.

"Mum had it done. Cancer."

Oh, shit.

"Fuck, I'm sorry."

"S'all right," Aled said, coming to lean in the kitchen doorway. "I'm guessing you just want to dodge the baby bullet, though?"

"Yeah. And I've heard it reduces mood swings." And random periods, though he wasn't as bothered about them as he used to be.

"And I'm guessing after your lovely experiences after headbutting a bus, you want to go private?"

Gabriel flipped him off, but nodded. "I'd prefer it."

Gabriel's experience of the NHS was uniformly negative. From the GP who'd outed him to his abusive mother to the nurses who'd placed him on a female ward after his car accident. He *hated* the NHS. Whenever he saw those 'save the NHS' protests, a savage and selfish part of him wanted to let it burn. If he wasn't allowed to have any dignity or help from the cunts, why should anyone else?

"Going by how much they fought to avoid giving me the hormones, I don't think getting something surgically removed is going to be any easier," he said. "And I'm fed up with having to prove I'm a bloke and not bonkers every time I talk to them. So yeah. If we have the savings, I'd rather just do it privately."

"See what we get for this place," Aled said. "And what prices they're asking for to get a decent house in St Ives."

"You want St Ives itself, then?"

"If we can afford it. Once we're all moved, we can look again at the savings and work something out. That sound okay?"

"More than. Thank you."

"No problem, sweetheart." Something sizzled and he retreated. "Extra cheese?"

"Duh," Gabriel replied, but curled his toes in his shoes at the casual support. Aled was a bit of a lummox when it came to gender stuff. He was so cis it was laughable. But Gabriel never minded, because of that simple, steady support. If Gabriel needed something, Aled would help him get it. He smiled at the brushes as he set them aside, and decided they could have a little fun later as a reward. Maybe Aled wouldn't be satisfied with his work and they could play.

Aled brought both enchiladas on a large plate and sat on the stairs with it on his knees, Gabriel sneaking forkfuls between passes with the rollers. They talked idly, slagging off a neighbour's parking skills. The pale green wall turned a bright white and, in no time at all, the first coat was done.

"It already looks better," Aled opined.

"Good."

"So what else is on your list?"

"Fresh coat of paint in every room," Gabriel said, getting out the brushes again to start lining the skirting board in the living room. "Fix the spare room door. New laminate in the kitchen—I'll ask Kevin to give me a hand with that. Hang some mirrors to make the rooms look bigger and brighter. Sort that bottom kitchen drawer…"

"Have you been watching *Homes Under the Hammer* again?"

"Not *recently*, but…"

Aled chuckled. "Honestly, thank you. It'll be a big help if you can get most of this sorted while I wrangle with the mortgage provider."

"Tell you what," Gabriel said. "You sort the sale, and I'll sort getting it *ready* for sale. How's that?"

"Deal," Aled said. "Though I'll give you a hand with the living room paint, or you'll not be getting to bed until midnight."

"I can do tha—"

"I have designs on you in that bed *before* midnight, thank you."

Gabriel flashed a grin over his shoulder. "You want to play?"

"Haven't decided yet," Aled replied.

He joined in with the painting once he'd washed up and changed into some scruffs, and soon the living room glowed the same fresh white as the hall. Gabriel made for the brushes again—why not add the kitchen and finish off the ground floor completely?—but his wrists were caught in paint-flecked hands and he was towed backwards into Aled's chest.

"Oh no you don't," Aled murmured, kissing his neck. "Told you. Designs. And we both have work in the morning, so let's put those plans into motion, hm?"

Gabriel grinned, squirming free. "Okay, okay. Let me wash them first, though."

Aled smacked him on the bum, propelling him towards the kitchen, but left him alone to clean up. He wandered off upstairs for a shower, and Gabriel turned the possibilities over in his head as he cleaned up. Definitely a game. He knew that predatory look a mile off. He was going to get *fucked*. But what kind to ask for? His arms ached from the rollers, so bondage wasn't going to be very good...

He still hadn't come to a decision when Aled came back down in his briefs to chivvy him along, biting again as they stood at the sink and rubbing hot hands around Gabriel's stomach to play with his belt.

"Come on," he insisted. "Bedtime."

"Mm, just—"

"*Bed.*"

Gabriel was towed backwards to the stairs, ending up on the bottom step with Aled's legs around his waist and both arms around his shoulders. The kiss on the back of the head was expected. The hands toying with the edges of his binder were *definitely* expected.

The question was not.

"Have you told Chris what we've decided yet?"

"Not yet," Gabriel admitted.

Another kiss grazed his ear.

"Can I ask you to bump that up your to-do list?"

"Okay."

"Do it tomorrow," Aled murmured. "Tonight, let me say thank you."

Gabriel shivered as the words washed over his ear. "H-how?"

"Any game you want," Aled whispered.

Gabriel curled his toes. His earlier ideas fled. *Any* game? He didn't have to think twice.

"I've been calling other men behind your back," he lied. "*Punish* me."

He could always call Chris in the afternoon, once his voice was better.

Chapter Nine

When Gabriel's number flashed up on his phone, Chris muted the movie.

"Hey."

"He-ey. So. News."

Chris sat up. "News?"

"Moving news."

Oh.

"You and Aled talked?"

"Yeah. He brought it up yesterday."

"And?"

Gabriel laughed. "So I was right."

"About?" Chris prompted.

"He wants the job that Tom offered, but he was terrified I was going to want to stay here, or I'd have a big alcoholic relapse if we moved and I was too far away from Kevin."

"I'm guessing you set him straight, then?" Chris said.

"Yeah. In a few ways that you don't like to hear the details of," Gabriel admitted. "But long story short, we're moving to St Ives."

Chris' jaw sagged. "That's it? You decided just like that? *Really?*"

He was honestly shocked. As much as Aled teased him about being emotionally overcautious, *Aled* was the overcautious one when it came to practical decisions like jobs and houses. It had taken them months to agree on a new place to live when Gabriel had wanted to sell up from the old house on Henry Street. Chris hadn't expected a decision just like that — and nothing so precise as the exact *town*.

"Yep!"

"Oh wow."

This changed things. He'd been hoping for just *closer*. Closer — anywhere closer — would have worked wonders. But St Ives itself —

"I could do that," he said.

Gabriel laughed again, sounding a little giddy. "Isn't it perfect?"

"That's — Jesus. *Wow.*"

"I know, right!"

"So — so like, how? Did you discuss us? Did — "

"Well, his best friend lives in St Ives so Aled is pitching for somewhere around there. He mentioned that first when we talked about it," Gabriel said. "But I don't know exactly how we'll arrange it yet. He did say he'd prefer separate houses."

"Honestly, me too. That stay was cramped."

"We could try for nearby, though?" Gabriel wheedled. "Like, same town at least? Walking distance?"

"Yeah, ideally," Chris said. His mind was spinning. No more long train journeys. No more elaborate planning around work. "I have an interested buyer for the bungalow already. One of Mum's neighbours. So...I'll probably be on the move first, right?"

"Probably. Aled has to give a month's notice anyway, and we need to spruce this house up a little bit first."

"So...I could always go job shopping in Penzance or somewhere," Chris said. "Find work and a flat. And then—it's just Cornwall, right? It's not that big. So, wherever you are, you won't be *too* far. And then we can work out a better nearby situation once you're here and we've all got a better idea of everything."

Gabriel made a shrill noise that might have been a squeal, but Chris knew better than to comment on it.

"I'm on it," Chris said. "I'll let you know what I find."

"Okay. Aled's going to ask Suze if she can find me work. Do you want her to look for you too?"

"Sure, I guess?"

"Send me your CV," Gabriel ordered.

Chris grimaced. "Uh. I'll make one. Okay. Let me—let me go and make one and book a few trips to go and hunt for work. I'll ring you back tomorrow."

"Okay. Love you!"

The excited sign-off made Chris grin goofily, and he switched off the TV before padding into his room for his laptop. He'd never really made a CV. He got jobs round Nailsea by knowing people. He wouldn't have any such advantage in Cornwall, so maybe it was time to get cracking.

Holy hell, he'd be living close enough to see Gabriel whenever they wanted.

His heart was beating a mile a minute as he set up job alerts and hunted for train tickets. He'd done a lot of jobs, both in and out of the army. He'd tended bars, cleaned offices, sold memberships. He'd even gotten a couple of NVQs before signing up to the army. Ryan would give him a good reference from the garage if he could find any chopshops hiring. And Cornwall was bound to be rammed with outdoors stores, right? Bike shops and sports clubs and all sorts. There'd be plenty to go round with his experience.

He could find a little flat in the town and cycle out to the villages whenever he liked. Gabriel could hop on the bus for half an hour and jump off for a hug at the end. They didn't have to plan every moment in advance. They could go for dinner after work. All go out together or Chris could steal Gabriel for himself for an evening. And get rid of him, too. When all that sexual energy was too much, he didn't need to feel guilty anymore. Aled would be a stone's throw away, not hundreds of miles. It wouldn't derail a visit anymore, because there'd always be tomorrow.

There'd be *every* tomorrow.

"Fuck," Chris said, and laughed to himself. "You're in bloody love."

It wasn't a revelation. It wasn't even much of a realisation. But he said it out loud in his late mother's bungalow, and it felt—for the first time—like he'd opened the closet door. He'd never breathed a word of his sexuality to her, terrified of her confirming that he was a freak after all, and she'd died without a clue, as far as Chris knew. She was dead and gone, and this was the first time he'd even hinted at it within these walls.

And yet—

She wasn't there to hear him anymore, but a tiny part of him felt as though he'd told her anyway.

* * * *

"You're kidding," Chris said.

The valuation agent chuckled.

She was a middle-aged woman from the local estate agent, and Chris had asked her to come and give him a rough idea of what he might get for selling Mum's bungalow. He'd expected her to poke around for ten minutes, give him a list of things wrong with the place, then say ninety or maybe even a hundred grand.

Not—

Well, not *that*.

"No, Mr Wheeler. And that's a mid-range estimate. It could easily be more if you follow some of my suggestions."

Chris made an embarrassing sort of gurgle. Her suggestions hadn't even been that much. Cleaning out the gutters. Repair that frozen stopcock. Normal stuff he'd planned on doing anyway. He wasn't exactly going to have to get a new roof to hit the figures she was quoting.

"Think it over," the agent said. "We'd love to take this one on. I'll give you a call in a couple of days to discuss the particulars."

She showed herself out, and Chris sat down in the armchair with a heavy, boneless *thunk*. The paper shook in his numb hand. Noodle slunk out from under the table and leapt up onto the arm of the chair with a curious chirp.

"Yeah," Chris muttered. "I can't believe it either."

After his chat with Gabriel, he'd figured he'd best get the bungalow valued. Just to see what he might have to work with. Just to see if he could afford a little flat or something, or if it'd be back into renting but with a nice savings buffer instead of the hand-to-mouth life he'd led since leaving the army.

He hadn't figured —

"Fuck," he muttered.

Noodle chirped again, then slunk onto his lap and began to turn in circles.

"We could afford something," he told the uninterested cat. "Fuck. I could — I have *money*."

His phone started buzzing in his back pocket, but it took a couple of goes before he could put down the estate agent's estimate. When he finally managed it, he slid the phone out to see Gabriel's smile flashing up at him.

"Er. Hey."

"Hey!" Gabriel sounded bright and cheerful, but it bounced off Chris' stunned thoughts. "You busy?"

"Uh. No. Not — no."

There was a short pause.

"Are you all right?"

"Yeah," Chris said. "Just a bit shellshocked."

"Why? What happened?"

"I had the estate agent round to value Mum's bungalow," Chris said.

"Oh, *no*, was it bad news?"

Chris barked a laugh. "Er. Not exactly."

"Good news?"

"I was thinking, you know, maybe I could get a hundred grand or so and use it to start over in Cornwall with you guys when you get round to moving."

"And?"

Chris could barely cough out the figure.

"Sorry, what?"

"Two hundred and twenty."

"Holy *shit*."

"Yeah," Chris whispered. "And that's — that's mid-range. She says I could get more if I just do a couple of little jobs around the place."

"Oh my God."

"And if I rent it out, she says I could get, like, a third of what the garage are paying me."

"Fuck," Gabriel said. "What are you going to do?"

"I've no idea," Chris confessed. "I'm not — I've never had any money. I have like twenty quid left until payday next week. I've no fucking clue. I mean — fuck, what do I *do*?"

The amount was just nonsense. A couple of grand blew Chris' mind. The idea that Aled's cars were worth twenty grand each, at a minimum, was staggering. But *two hundred and twenty thousand pounds*?

It just — it wasn't a real number. The valuer might as well have said he was sitting on a million. It was nonsense.

Something banged in the background, and a lightbulb came on in Chris' head. *He* might not know what to do, and Gabriel didn't come from any better stock when it came to money stuff, but they both knew someone who did.

"Is Aled there?"

"Yeah, he took a half-day at work. Meeting with the mortgage people. S'Chris," Gabriel added in a muffled aside. Chris heard a brief kiss then something about the microwave.

"Put me on speaker?" Chris asked. "I don't know any other rich fucks."

Gabriel snorted with laughter. The odd echo of speakerphone clicked in, then Gabriel yelled, "Aled! Chris wants some financial advice!"

Background noise reigned for a short while—the trundle of their noisy washing machine, footsteps, the low chatter of a TV—then leather creaked and a sharp slap sounded. Chris surmised that Aled had sat down, and Gabriel had tried to put his feet in his lap before being rejected.

"What's up, Chris?"

Chris bottled his confusion up into a few jumbled sentences, feeling simultaneously a touch foolish—who didn't like getting told they had more money than they'd thought?—but also a little reassured. Aled had a calming presence, and Chris had let him into far more personal shit than his house valuation.

"Congratulations," Aled said. "I guess the first thing is to decide what you actually want to do with it."

"I was figuring I'd sell it."

"To be honest, I'd say it's the better move. Unless you can build a property portfolio, renting out one property isn't usually worth it, with all the rules and regulations these days."

Chris wondered what the hell a property portfolio was.

"What do you want to sell it *for*, then?" Aled asked. "I mean, do you want to buy somewhere else in cash, with no mortgage to pay off? Or are you wanting to use the funds for something else and get a mortgage or go back to renting?"

Well, at least he knew *that* bit.

"Can't very well commute from Nailsea to Cornwall," Chris remarked.

Aled coughed. "Gabriel's told you the plan then?"

"Yeah. I mean, I know you've got your place and shit, but I figured — you know, I can do whatever. Get a job in a shop or something. I was thinking I could get myself set up sooner rather than later and then I'll be there already by the time you guys arrive."

"Aye," Aled said. "But did he tell you what he wants about living arrangements?"

"Er —"

"Close!" Gabriel chipped in. "Next door or down the road!"

"Or, with two hundred grand to spare, an annexe," Aled said.

"Eh?" Chris said. "Start over. Close what?"

"I want all three of us to live close together," Gabriel said. "So I can just come home from work and be like, oh hey, let's go to Chris' and your front door is only a short walk from Aled's. If that."

"Um. No offence, but —"

"Don't worry," Gabriel said. "Aled already vetoed a big studio flat together."

Chris laughed, relieved. "Good."

"But I want you close by," Gabriel insisted. "Really close."

"Other option is a granny annexe," Aled said. "Separate buildings, same plot of land."

It clicked.

"Oh. Oh, I get it. You think we could find somewhere like that? And buy it together?"

"I can get four hundred grand on a mortgage," Aled said. "You're sitting on another two hundred. For that, we can try to find a house with a granny annexe, or one with enough land to build one. All we'd have to do is pool our financial resources. And, to be frank, I should make *another* seventy grand or so by selling this place, so between us, that's a big budget. We'd have plenty of space from each other, but equal access to this demanding shit."

Judging by the sudden grunt, the demanding shit in question had slugged him in the gut.

"Bastard," Gabriel groused.

Chris ignored them, stuck on the maths. Two hundred and twenty for Mum's bungalow. Four hundred that Aled could borrow. Seventy extra from the house in Newmillardam.

"That's...that's...um...seven hundred and ten?" he guessed.

"Six hundred and ninety," Aled corrected gently.

"I was close."

"Closer than this princess. Ow! Lay off!"

"Stop insulting me then!"

Chris snickered and waited for Aled to get control again. Another couple of smacks and a grumble later, peace was restored.

"I don't know how much things cost in St Ives," he said.

"I did a quick look. Six hundred and ninety can definitely get us somewhere decent, even in the posh areas of Cornwall. Just depends on availability. Whether anyone is selling what we want where we want it."

"Wait," Gabriel interrupted. "Are we agreeing to one plot of land, then? So Chris is *right there*?"

"I hadn't really thought about it," Chris admitted. "But it's not a bad idea."

He liked Aled fine, but living together might be a bit much. Chris was shy, and Aled was used to starting sex games wherever the hell he wanted. And much as Chris was discovering his own boundaries weren't as solid and impassable as he'd thought, he wasn't up for seeing Aled in the all-together too often.

Plus, he couldn't imagine St Ives was full of thugs, but an annexe would keep Gabriel's middle-of-the-night wanderings between boyfriends to a safer minimum. He said as much, and was threatened with a slap of his own.

"You're both shits," Gabriel complained.

"So you *wouldn't* like to be able to just wander across the garden and let yourself into Chris' house?" Aled mocked.

"I didn't say that."

Chris grinned, warming to the idea.

"Tell you what," Aled said. "Get your place on the market, *don't* accept anything less than two twenty for it, and let me know a Friday or Saturday you're free. I'll book some viewings at some likely properties, and we can meet up, go house shopping, have a few pints if this one's working."

Gabriel grumbled but didn't raise a proper protest. Chris presumed he had a run of weekends at the gym. But—much as it would be odd to go somewhere with just Aled and no Gabriel—it might be fun, too.

"It's a date," he said. "How about the seventeenth?"

Chapter Ten

Aled didn't get much sleep that night.

He wasn't a natural risk-taker, and he'd lived his whole life in this tiny corner of West Yorkshire. He'd only moved out of his parents' house to go to university, and even then he'd not gone further than Huddersfield.

But his parents were gone, their ashes long since scattered over their beloved Dales. Nan had slipped away quietly in her sleep, a gentle end to a long and loving life. His best friend and pseudo-sister was at the other end of this idea to move. And his biggest fear – that Gabriel would want to stay – had been cut out from under him.

Aled could handle the condition. He liked Chris. They'd essentially lived together for a while after Gabriel's accident last year. He'd rather they had their own space, but an annexe or opposite sides of a street had a nice appeal. And house-sharing in the short term wasn't a problem.

He ought to just accept the offer. The pay cut was significant, but it was still more than enough to live comfortably. Gabriel could easily find work in one of the hotels. Cornwall was beautiful.

Yet-yet-yet—

"Aled," a voice grumbled from the vicinity of his armpit. "Turn your brain off or take it somewhere else."

He rolled his eyes, but it was already ten past six. So he slipped out of bed and took his brain to the bathroom.

The hot water beating down on the back of his neck in the shower shook off the cobwebs and provided a little inspiration. He was being too *Aled* about it all. He needed to be a little more like Gabriel, who went with the flow of life rather than trying to really navigate it. And where would this current take him, if he just lay back in the water and floated?

A house in Cornwall with his partner, his sister and her family just up the road, a job and a smaller car.

He could suddenly see it. Gabriel faking that his knee hurt to avoid babysitting. Being forced into cycling to Lizard Point instead of driving like a normal person. A cottage. Flowers in the front garden. Resuming the birthday drinks tradition, and Gabriel coming back from Chris' in the morning to make fun of his hangover.

The mental image played out in his head as he got ready for work. Gabriel put in a rumpled appearance once the toast popped, then vanished again for his own shower. He came into the bedroom, wet and tempting as always, while Aled was doing his tie, but they mutually ignored each other until the majority of skin on both sides of the bed was covered.

Then Gabriel crossed the divide, leaned up for a kiss, and said, "Call Tom."

"You know me that well?"

"Yep. Already told Chris."

"So what's my answer?"

"Yes. Chris is going to look into moving to Penzance in the short term. Just a suggestion for you when it comes to locations."

Aled chuckled, and offered another kiss.

"Last chance to object."

"Nope."

"Going once…"

"Still no."

"Going twice…"

"I'm off work at four so I'll start dinner. Lasagne sound good?"

"Sold to Cornwall, I guess. And yeah, sounds nice."

Gabriel went off downstairs, and Aled unplugged his phone from the charger to call Tom before he set off—only to smirk at the waiting text message.

Kevin: Any plans with Gabriel tonight?

Probably not lasagne, if Kevin was up for some fun.

Me: Nope

Kevin: So he's free for a kidnapping then?

Me: No objection on my part. He's working eight four at the gym.

Kevin: On his bike?

"Want a lift to work?" Aled shouted.

"No thanks! Okay, I'm off."

"See you later."

"Later, love you!"

"Love you too."

Me: Yup

Kevin: Cheers

Me: Let me know if you want to keep him overnight.

Kevin: Will do mate

Aled went down to take a pizza out to defrost before leaning up against the counter and calling Tom. His mobile rang out, so he tried the landline and got Suze, with a chatty background of Euan.

"Hey, Suze. Has Tom gone to work already?"

"No, he's just getting out the shower. Is it about the job? Are you going to say yes?"

Aled cracked a smile, then held the phone at arm's length and shouted, "Yes!"

She screamed. Even at a distance, it was deafening. Aled put the phone back to his ear with a laugh, just in time to hear her yelling the news at Tom up the stairs.

"What's he say?" Aled asked.

"About fu—about time. And to text him your leaving date. Oh, and if accommodation is a problem then you can always use one of the hotels for a couple of weeks."

"Thanks. Can you put out some feelers for Gabriel?"

"Has he done receptionist work before?"

"Does it at the gym twice a week."

"Okay. There's usually some temp stuff during the holiday season. No bar work, right?"

"Yeah."

"Get him to send me his CV and I'll see what I can find."

"Thanks, Suze. You're a star."

"I'll put in some calls about a short-term let, too. It's pretty limited in St Ives—are you both okay with renting in Penzance or Plymouth for a little bit until you can do some proper house shopping?"

"Long as nobody gets gay-bashed, I don't care. Though might just park Gabriel up with Chris. Nobody would dare."

"Still looks like he stomps on kittens for fun?"

"Yup."

"So he's coming too?"

"Yeah but I think he's sorting his own place to stay."

"Fine, but you tell him, if he wants any help, give me a call."

"You're a star."

"Of course I am! You're coming home! You'll be here in time for the baby."

In the background, Euan made his opinion of the imminent baby clear, much as Aled doubted he understood any of it at his age.

"I doubt we'll quite make it, but we'll definitely be round the corner when you drop numbers three through five."

"Good. We miss you. Both of you. Now go and tell Foster!"

Aled hung up with a laugh, then texted her some kisses before pushing off from the counter and grabbing his keys off the hook. For the first time since she'd left, he felt happy going to work. Christ. He'd call himself slow on the uptake, but then it had taken him over a year of not setting eyes on his wife to accept that his marriage was over. He'd never been so good at dealing with his issues.

But there was no denying he'd made the right choice. The air smelled better. The traffic wasn't annoying. Having to do fifty-six adjustments to park beside Mitchell's obviously abandoned car in the office car park was irrelevant.

He was going home.

West Yorkshire had been home for his whole life, like a worn jumper that smelled familiar. It wasn't flattering or good-looking, but it fit just right and kept out the cold and the damp. But that had been with his grandmother, his parents, his best friend, his partner. It had been about the people in his life. Home was where they were.

And some were just memories, which he carried everywhere he went. Some were down south. And one would be coming with him.

"Morning, Frank." He nodded to the security guard. "Mr Foster showed up yet?"

"Hey, Aled. Sure did, about twenty minutes ago. You're in a good mood. Happy wife?"

"Happy life!"

He stopped off to drop his briefcase in his office before continuing up to the top floor and the corridor of power. Of course, most of the occupants didn't waltz in until half eleven, then turned straight back round and went out for a three-hour working lunch. Aled had chased the final promotion to get him that lifestyle. Now it just seemed pathetic.

Arthur Foster's office was lit like a beacon at the end of the gloomy corridor, though, and Aled rapped his knuckles on the door before poking his head around it.

"Got a minute, sir?"

Arthur Foster was ancient. A bald wisp of a man, it was well-known that he refused to retire because he and his wife hated each other but were too stuck in their ways to call it a day. Several thought he'd die in the job. Aled was one of them. And with him hunched behind the enormous desk, prodding the computer like it might explode...that day was probably not too far away.

"Come in, come in. Have a seat. You've not seen that bloody email from Mitchell, have you?"

"Not yet, sir. Haven't logged on. I have some news and I wanted you to be the first to know."

"Oh?"

"I'm resigning."

Foster paused. He sat back. The chair groaned. He removed his glasses and squinted at Aled as though he'd never seen him before.

"Resigning."

"Yes, sir."

"Headhunted?"

"In a manner of speaking, sir."

"Well, if it's money and a benefits package, there'll be no argument from the board about—"

"We don't have an office in Cornwall, sir."

"Ah. Location."

"Yes, sir."

"Why?"

"I want to be closer to my family, sir."

Foster nodded. He steepled his fingers like a villain from one of Gabriel's bad films, and kept nodding.

"I see."

"I can send an official email."

"Best for — for HR, yes."

Aled clicked his tongue. "Well, uh, if you'll excuse me — "

"Hold on a moment. The board won't like it, you know. They were discussing you taking over Campbell's post at the end of the year already."

"My mind is made up, sir."

To his surprise, Foster's reply was, "Good."

"Er. Sir?"

"Life's too damn short to waste time working and not seeing your family enough. Otherwise you wake up old with two strangers in your house for Christmas and you've no idea who your wife is."

Ouch.

"Um — "

"Good on you. If you get too much bullshit from them, you let me know."

"Thank you, sir."

"Send your official resignation to me and copy Linda in HR into it. Get the ball rolling before this afternoon's nap with the accounting guys."

"Will do."

"And, Aled?"

"Yes, sir?"

"Congratulations."

"Er — "

"The mood you're in? I know baby news when I see it."

Aled coughed a laugh, then decided to just go with it. "Thank you, sir."

He fired off a text to Suze before he even reached the lifts, then another to Gabriel as he waited for one to arrive.

Me: Just resigned. And apparently I'm walking around looking giddy as a new father, so congratulations.

Chapter Eleven

As Gabriel slowed at the quiet junction, a grubby Transit van pulled up alongside him. Worn livery advertised *Kevin's Kit ens & Bat rooms* in pink, maybe formerly red, lettering. The driver that leaned out of the open window was a tall, muscular black man with long dreads pulled back into a low ponytail. He grinned, and a gold tooth flashed.

"Help a brother out?" he said. "I'm looking for Henry Street."

Gabriel raised his eyebrows. He used to live on Henry Street with Aled.

"Never heard of it."

"I got a map." The driver got out. The van rocked as he slammed the door, then he opened the back and waved shabby paper at Gabriel. "See? Only I'm no good at these."

"Uh, okay," Gabriel said. He propped his bike up against a garden wall and walked round to the back of the van. "So do you know roughly where — *hey*!"

A hand seized his elbow. Another his waistband. He was bodily lifted into the van, the man at his back. Gabriel's knees hit the floor. The door banged shut, and for a moment there was nothing but the dark.

"Let me out!"

"Maybe later."

A torch flickered into life. A boot hit him in the back and held him down. Something ripped. Tape was pressed over his mouth, and his wrists were bound behind his back. Then he was dragged up by the shoulders and slammed into a seat.

"Safety first."

The clunk of the seatbelt was deafening. The torch went out. In the dark, thick fingers stroked his palms.

Kevin. Not the persona of a stranger. Kevin, checking like always.

Gabriel spread his hands open. If gagged, the safeword was to clench a fist. If it was dark, it became snapping his fingers — but there was no way he was safewording such a promising scene.

Kevin nodded — and the act resumed.

"Sit tight, slut. Be plenty for you to do later."

The door slammed again. After a brief pause, it opened and Gabriel's bike was rigged to the wall before another slam, more darkness and the grind of a lock. The engine chugged into life, then the van did a rough U-turn and headed back up the hill.

Gabriel didn't bother trying to track the van's movements. If Kevin was going to use toys or get creative, they'd go to his house. He didn't really play anywhere else. If he was just going to get fucked on the floor of the van, they might go anywhere. A country lane with nobody to hear him scream, or a busy high street with shoppers only inches away.

Which would he prefer?

He decided on a country lane—trying to be quiet while being fucked with Kevin's truncheon of a cock wasn't sexy, it was just impossible—and got lucky. The roads got worse. The van jolted. Tyres crunched on gravel, then dirt, then fell silent as the van rolled over soft hillocks of grass or sandy earth.

The engine died. The van dipped. Kevin hawked and spat before closing the door. His steps were silent, and Gabriel closed his eyes only just in time to avoid being blinded when the back doors were flung open.

For a while, Kevin didn't say a word. The van was full of tools, but he snapped open a briefcase that Gabriel knew very well from previous kidnappings, and set everything up how he wanted. A collar and chain around Gabriel's throat, the end of the chain padlocked around the towbar hinge under the back bumper. A picnic blanket spread out on the grass in the evening sun. A vial was unscrewed and a needle drawn up, the drug shimmering in the gold light.

"Just a little relaxant," he said. "Make you nice and pliant."

It stung. He taped a plaster over the site mockingly, then took Gabriel's jaw in one massive hand and looked him dead in the eye.

"Let's get a couple of things clear," he said. "We're going to be out here a while, and I'm going to fuck you. How is up to you. You take that tape off your mouth, that means you want to blow me. You come when I'm fingering you, that means you want my dick where my hand was. You turn your back on me, that's an invite into your arse. You resist me, that just means you want it rougher. Understood?"

Gabriel nodded.

"Good."

The seatbelt was removed, then the tape around Gabriel's wrists. Then his clothes. It was a brisk but intimate strip—his tits were sucked as his binder was removed, his arse was massaged once his shorts were halfway down his legs, his cunt fingered once his briefs had been yanked off. Once naked, he was dragged to the van doors by the chain and shoved out, stumbling onto the blanket. They were in a meadow. Long grass flowed up the side of a stubby hill to a dark treeline, silhouetted by the setting sun. He could make it, as long as he ran before the drugs kicked in.

The chain jerked him back to reality. Sitting on the edge of the van floor, Kevin reeled him in until Gabriel was dragged up to straddle his thighs, the bulge in Kevin's trousers jutting up between them. When Kevin pulled down the zip, his monstrous cock sprang free immediately.

"Nice, isn't it? Even you'd struggle to handle all of this at once. Come on. Play with it. It wants to play with you, after all."

A hand on his arse pulled him closer as Gabriel wrapped a hand around the immense girth of it. He couldn't close his fingers all the way. It twitched and hardened even more as he clumsily jacked it, and trying to ignore the way Kevin was sucking on his nipple, the thumb that had been shoved dry into his arse, the wet heat pooling in his cunt.

But he couldn't figure out how to run. He was chained like a dog. The hand opening his arse meant he couldn't pull back. The teeth on his breast wouldn't let go. And Kevin pushing him up, up onto his knees, guiding that leaking head to his cunt, ready to—

Gabriel's hand began to shake.

The drug was kicking in. If he wanted to be chased, he had to act fast. If he wanted that conquering in the grass, it had to be now.

He pulled his hand away from Kevin's cock and ripped the tape from his mouth.

"You little whore," Kevin laughed. "Knew you couldn't resist."

Gabriel slipped down from his lap and kissed the head. His knees were wobbling. He drooled on the meat in his mouth before he managed to suck it.

And his fingers scrabbled at the collar.

Kevin had tipped his head back. Sighing at the sky. Gabriel sucked desperately as he worked the buckle with sweaty fingers.

Come on, come on, let go –

It broke free, and Gabriel *ran*.

"Hey!"

He bolted. Straight for the hill. Fast as he could.

Only –

Too late. His knees buckled with every blow. His lungs reeled. The hillside tipped. The sky turned green. He forced himself up again, but only make it a handful of dizzy steps before he tipped again. His arms shook as he tried again.

Someone chuckled.

"My fault for untying you, I suppose."

A hand swiped his ribs. He fell. Kevin loomed over him – shirtless, belt in hand, massive cock jutting from his open fly like a shelf.

"Very nice," he said, pushing Gabriel's legs apart with his boot and nudging his vagina. "You turned your back on me."

Gabriel cringed, shaking his head.

"Oh yes you did. But I'll get to that later. Wait until that relaxant wears off. More of a punishment then."

He slid down and over Gabriel like a hungry snake, pushing weak limbs aside until Gabriel was hopelessly exposed. Cupping his jaw once more, Kevin held eye contact as he pushed in. His cock was immense. Endless. It burned like the surface of the sun. Gabriel clenched and it kept going anyway. He could do nothing but take it — yet how *could* he take it? It was like being fisted. Too much, too dry, too sudden —

"There we go," Kevin whispered.

It stopped. Right up against the danger zone, it stopped. He felt so full that his guts ached. His lungs struggled to inflate all the way. It pushed at *everything*.

"What a welcoming little cunt you have," Kevin whispered.

The kiss was filthy. Plundering. Defiling. And just as Gabriel ran out of air, the cock inside him *surged*, and another two inches were forced inside him. He wrenched his head away, but it was wrenched right back and he was kissed again. Another surge. Another silenced cry of anguish.

Then it stopped barely short of his cervix, and Kevin smiled down at him with a terrifying hunger.

"If I were you, I'd stay nice and still."

Gabriel nodded.

"If you look away," Kevin breathed, "I'll bottom out."

The earth tipped, and it wasn't the drug. He could. He was long enough. He'd hit Gabriel's cervix like a battering ram, and the pain would make him vomit until he blacked out. He'd never done it, but they both knew he could.

"But if you relax and behave, there's no reason" — he slid out to the tip, then surged back like the unstoppable force of an incoming tide — "you can't enjoy it too."

The relaxant was sinking in. Every thrust was long and slow, like a boat being gently towed through a still lake. Gabriel's whole body shuddered with the impact. He rippled like water, the pinch of a hard hand in his hair the only thing anchoring him to the swaying world.

"Did you think this was a one-time thing?" Kevin whispered. "I'd take you and rape you and put you back?"

The soft tone, the almost vanilla fuck, but the cruel words were a drug all of their own. Gabriel flexed and felt wet heat pooling inside.

"Look at you, getting wet and milking my dick like that. You're the perfect little whore. Let me take all your clothes off without a fuss. Asked to suck my dick so politely. Wriggled around on my lap, absolutely gagging for it."

Gabriel whimpered as the first warning ripple flowed over his abdomen. He was close, dangerously close.

"Lying there, good as gold and taking it. And that mouth — that's perfect. Those lips sucking on me is going to be a daily thing. Your breakfast for the rest of your life. First thing you'll do when you wake up is kiss my dick hello."

Kevin's eyes were right there —

"You'll be begging me to fuck you by the end of the week."

This cock, his fingers, his eyes, his voice —

"I own you."

Lightning struck him. He seized. Screamed into the mouth that sealed his own. Shook. Was that the world? Was it him? Who — what —

Who.

What.

Gabriel blinked.

Dark hair swayed around him in long ropes like curtains. Breath panted. Fingers like claws in his hips. His ribs were jerking. His cunt —

He clenched.

"Fuuuuuuck."

His aching cunt was flooded. His skin was slick. Lips grazed his own. Something pulled out of him in a hot, slippery rush.

"Ow —"

Hard fingers in his pussy. Jabbing. Poking.

"Get up."

The body that had held him down rose, but Gabriel couldn't tell which way was up. His limbs refused to move. Hands dragged him up by the wrists and he collapsed into Kevin's frame, wet as a kitten. The kiss forced into his mouth was still hungry. He was lifted higher, legs opened around Kevin's waist, and their combined climaxes flooded from his cunt in a revolting betrayal.

"We're going to go back to our blanket," Kevin said as he walked through the grass. "You're going to put your collar back on. Then you're going to suck my dick until it's ready for your arse. The drugs will be wearing off by then. So I will turn you over and I will really rape you. I will make you scream. I will make you bleed. I will fuck you so you can't walk, never mind run from me again. And then we can go home. Understood?"

The blanket was scratchy. Kevin's cock was soft and familiar, sex and cum all mixed together. He held Gabriel's head and neck in both hands and massaged his own dick with Gabriel's mouth like an expert.

But—

But—

Something wasn't right.

Where they still in the meadow? It was cold. Who was fingering him? His fingers spasmed. He couldn't move. He couldn't think. Oh God—

"Hey."

It was too much. His body wasn't his. He was drifting away. There was nothing here, nothing—

"Colour?"

The words were rubbery. His tongue numb. There was nothing in his mouth anymore. Someone was stroking his hair.

It bubbled over like a boiling pot, and Gabriel burst into tears.

"*Red.* Oh fuck, red-red-red—"

"Whoa, whoa, whoa, okay. Okay, angel. Okay. It's all right, I heard you. Red. Game over."

Blanket. Arms. Warmth. Kevin's legs under his. His heart pounding in Gabriel's ear.

"Ssh, angel. I've got you. It's all right."

"S'too strong. I'm so—I don't—nothing's working—"

"That's all right. I've got you. Nobody else here. Just you and me."

"Just you, just you, just you…"

"That's right, just me."

A heavy hand was stroking his hair and the side of his face. Gabriel clung. The world was spinning. He felt like water draining away to nothingness.

"Close your eyes. Now breathe in. Nice and deep. Hold. And out. Good. That's very good. Again. Iiiin…"

He breathed. The sense of dissolving eased. His brain started to come back online. He curled his limbs tighter, and Kevin's arms followed.

Kevin's lap. Wrapped in the picnic blanket. A warm finger tracing the shell of his ear, over and over.

"What's happening?" he whispered.

"I think you spaced a little but the drug made you panic."

"It feels so strong."

"Same amount we've used before, angel."

"P-promise?"

A kiss pushed against his scalp.

"When have I ever used something on you we haven't agreed to before?"

"Never."

"Exactly. I used exactly the same stuff in the same amount as last time. And I won't be doing it again. Not if it's giving you a funny turn."

Gabriel exhaled and opened his eyes. The world was brown and red. Kevin's skin and the blanket. Nothing else.

"I don't—it's—I—"

"It's all right," Kevin murmured. "Take your time. Did you eat before leaving work?"

"N-no."

"When was lunch?"

"Eleven."

"Ahh, that might be it."

"M'sorry—"

"Nothing to be sorry for." His voice was low and soothing. Gabriel closed his eyes, trying to burrow into the sound. It was Kevin. Kevin was safe. Even as the panic clawed against the insides of his skull, another part of him recognised that Kevin was *safe*.

"Clothes. Please."

He needed the armour.

"No problem. Just relax. I'm going to carry you to the front seat, all right?"

Kevin's voice was a soft, patient murmur. He talked through every action. His hands were firm but gentle, and when they weren't helping Gabriel into his clothes or turning on the heater or fiddling with the seat, they were smoothing down his skin, pressing affection and love over the roleplayed abuse.

"It was going so well," Gabriel said miserably.

It was already starting to wear off — either the panic attack or the drug itself. He felt almost hungover.

"Tell me what happened."

"I came. Like…like an out-of-body experience. It was — just — God, it was one of the best I've ever had. But then when I came back, it was like my whole body wasn't mine. Like I didn't know you or what was happening and I couldn't do anything. And it was terrifying. Really terrifying, not — not the good thrill, but this awful horror. Like it was real."

Kevin stroked back his hair with both hands and leaned in to kiss the bridge of his nose.

"And then you safeworded," he whispered, "and I stopped."

"No."

Eyebrows rose. "Pardon?"

"You stopped before. You noticed something was wrong. You wanted a colour."

"True, but I was wondering if you were going to be sick, to be honest."

Gabriel laughed weakly. His body still felt rubbery and not quite his. But the panic had yielded to a miserable half-shame. He wasn't sure which he preferred.

"Okay. Here's my idea. You need looking after. So you can either come home with me and join us for dinner, or I can take you back home and walk you right into Aled's hands. Your choice, but you need someone who knows how to look after you so those are the only choices."

Gabriel squeezed his wrist. "Dinner sounds good. I have news anyway."

"Yeah? You good if I let go and pack up, or you need more time?"

"I'm okay."

He still felt wobbly and wrung-out, but the van was warm. He felt safe again. When Kevin got into the driver's seat, he leaned over for a kiss and there was a flicker of fresh arousal.

"We can do that some other time without the drugs, right?"

"Sure. In a few days, once you've had time to get back on an even keel. So what's this news?"

The engine chugged into life and Kevin wrestled the van out of the meadow and into a country lane. Stars were coming out on the horizon. Gabriel texted Aled his whereabouts—though no doubt Kevin had already done it after the kidnap—then spread his legs out into the footwell.

"Aled and I are moving."

"Again?"

"To Cornwall."

Kevin flexed his fingers on the wheel and blew out his cheeks.

"Christ," he said eventually. "What's brought that on?"

"He's been offered a job with a hotel chain, and his best friend lives in St Ives. He's been unsettled — unhappy — since she moved."

Kevin nodded. "Well, not like you aren't the moving kind."

Gabriel smiled. He was from London. Had grown up there. Then he'd fled a violently transphobic family and come north. He'd lived in Sheffield for a while, then Leeds after a relationship breakdown, then moved in with Aled in Wakefield.

Yet this felt different.

"First time I'll be leaving someone behind that I love."

Kevin snorted. "It's Cornwall, not Australia."

"Yeah. I'm still going to miss you and Judith and the kids, though."

"I would have been worried, once."

Gabriel rolled his head on the rest to frown at Kevin's profile in the dark.

"Once?"

"Yeah. All that way, nobody but your partner, no job, new home…a few years ago, I'd have tried to talk you out of it."

"And now?"

"You'll be fine."

Gabriel smiled.

"Be some new rules, though," Kevin said. "You're still family. Every six weeks, I'll send you the tickets and you'll get on the northbound train. No exceptions. You got it?"

Gabriel grinned as a heavy hand squeezed his knee and tucked the edge of the blanket under his chin.

"Yes, sir."

Chapter Twelve

Aled had another new car.

It pulled up just after six on Friday evening. Another Range Rover, but a rich blue instead of the previous black one.

"Do you get a new car every month?" Chris asked as he got in.

"Company car," Aled said. "Be a Ford Focus after this move, and second-hand at that."

They'd arranged a weekend of house-hunting in St Ives, but Gabriel hadn't been able to join them. Surprisingly, Chris hadn't minded much. They'd talked over the ads by phone, and Gabriel had insisted on coming to see whichever one they picked for himself before they signed any contracts. Submitting an offer was acceptable. Actually signing on the dotted line was not.

"Do you want to stop for anything?" Chris asked. "Loo break? Drink?"

"Nah. Stopped at Birmingham for a slash," Aled said. He nodded at the *For Sale* sign as he turned around in Chris' cul-de-sac. "Estate agent were fast with that, weren't they?"

"Arrived this morning," Chris said. "I signed on the dotted line yesterday after I was done at work. They've put it online at two hundred and thirty."

"Nice."

Chris shrugged. "Figured I might as well get a bit more, right?"

"Definitely," Aled said. "I don't know what it's like here, but where we live, bungalows often get into bidding wars."

"Into what?"

"When buyers compete with each other to win it. It's good for you. Means you'll get more money if that happens."

"Oh," Chris said. "I'm just going to stick to her original two hundred and twenty estimate. That's what we'll need, right?"

"Yep. Probably not that much, though. Did you get a good look at the ads I sent you? Most expensive is six fifty."

The intimidatingly expensive ads with large, luxurious houses that Chris had never in a million years even bothered to look at, never mind entertain a fantasy of buying? The *cheapest* had been four hundred thousand. That amount of money just blew his mind.

"Yeah, but I've never bought a house before. I haven't got a clue what I'm looking for."

And even if he did have practice, he'd never have been looking at properties with summerhouses and underfloor heating anyway. At most, the odd time he'd gone hunting for bedsits or roommates, he'd looked at whether the windows were double glazed.

"Well, what do you like to do in the house? You into cooking or gardening or anything like that?"

"I'd like to start gardening."

"There you go," Aled said. "Insist on decent outdoor space. That's one thing to look for."

"I guess," Chris said doubtfully.

"Don't worry about it," Aled said. "I've plenty of practice in that area. Just see if you like it."

"I've got low standards," Chris admitted. "Always lived in bedsits and shit until my mum died."

"I get it," Aled replied. "My student flat was a right shocker. And my ex-wife always used to moan at me that I was more worried about being able to afford a nice car than a nice house."

Chris was appreciating the nice car, though. It purred. He stretched out in the roomy passenger seat and found a suitable radio station as Aled rejoined the M5. The southbound traffic was reasonable, and Aled proved that he cared very little about speeding tickets, swerving into the fast lane within minutes and zooming off at a speed usually reserved for racetracks. Chris decided not to worry about it. Instead, they swapped small talk, mainly about Gabriel, until Aled gestured to the glovebox and said there was a wishlist.

"He's excited," Aled continued as Chris rummaged. "Spent all morning on that."

"Oh Christ."

The list was not only neat—and Gabriel usually had appalling handwriting—but colour-coded into the traffic light system usually reserved for sex safewords.

"I'm guessing red is the must-haves?"

"Yep."

There were only two red things—a place for Gabriel's bike, and a bathtub. The rest were a mixture of eye-bleeding orange and fetid green. Chris' brain hurt just looking at it.

"Apparently it needs at least five orange and two greens," Aled said. "And if there's nowhere to put the hammock then it's going to be a *really* hard sell. And he wants photos. So you can tick 'em off and take the pictures if you're not sure what you're after."

"Sure," Chris said.

He studied it as they cruised towards Cornwall, curious both about what Gabriel wanted in a home, and about what Chris was supposed to be looking for. Why was the boiler age important? Who cared what kind of wood the floor was made of? Couldn't they just replace the carpets if none of them were blue? Very little of it made sense — and very little of it was a part of Gabriel he'd seen before. Muddy mountain biking was clearly a very different kind of hobby from house-buying.

It was dark when they reached St Ives, and Aled seemed to have fobbed off his friends, for which Chris felt guiltily grateful. Instead, they had dinner and a couple of pints in the hotel bar, watching the football on the telly. Neither of them had much interest in the sport, and they flipped a coin to pick teams. Aled's lost. Gabriel texted just as Aled went to get another round in, punishment of losers the world over, and Chris chuckled when he saw the message.

Gabriel: You guys having fun? ;) x

Chris smiled. Surprisingly…

Me: Yep x

* * * *

Chris went for a run in the morning as usual.

The hotel was right in the middle of St Ives, just shy of the seafront. The salty air was refreshing and he took the opportunity to explore without being blindingly obvious. Several people were out walking dogs in the early morning. He wondered if a woman out with a buggy and a noisy baby was Aled's friend Suze. The tide was high but the sea calm. Boats bobbed quietly in the bay.

He could get used to that.

Aware that they had a busy day, Chris didn't stop out long. A short run of only four miles later, he jogged up the stairs to the hotel room and let himself back in to find Aled making coffee in his underwear, phone jammed between his shoulder and his ear.

"I don't *care* if Mitchell thinks it's emergency—"

Chris left him to it.

By the time he'd showered, whatever work emergency had been drummed up was gone. Aled offered him a cup, then ducked into the en suite for a quick shower of his own. And, thanks to no Gabriel, they were on their way in half an hour.

Thanks to Aled, to a local café.

Aled hadn't cleaned up his diet, and insisted on a bacon sandwich before they got going. Chris rolled his eyes and opted for a protein bar, but eventually they were on the move, the car stinking up of second coffees and greasy dead pig as Aled wrestled their way through narrow old roads and out to the first property.

Aled had booked viewings at four houses, all of which blew Chris' mind on paper alone. Mum had bought her bungalow back in the seventies with her then-hubby. When he'd disappeared with his secretary, Mum had screwed him out of the house in the divorce.

That was the only reason they'd ever had one. So gawping up at the enormous red-bricks squatting at least thirty yards back from the road behind manicured lawns and private gates, Chris wondered if he wasn't hallucinating.

"You're *sure* this is within our price range?"

"Yep. Come on. Let's see if we get a hard sell."

The estate agent was at least mildly homophobic, going by the startled expression at the sight of them followed by an insistence on calling them 'boys' despite the glaringly obvious fact that Aled was well over a decade older than him. So Chris was treated to the amusing sight of Aled's cold and pompous act, the same arsehole he'd played with the doctors when Gabriel had been in hospital. Chris rather enjoyed it — as long as it was directed at someone else.

The house was a bit of a bust — Chris knew enough after doing up Mum's bungalow to know they'd have to spend a fortune on the so-called annexe to make it habitable — but he enjoyed Aled baiting the agent and his insistence on knowing about the quality of the local schools even though none of them had any intention of having kids.

The second place was decent, with a better agent, and Chris ticked off enough of Gabriel's demands — bathtub, bike shed, roomy loft conversion that could become a playroom — but he still had no idea what he was supposed to think. A house was a house was a house, surely? Four walls. Roof. Front door with lock. Done. Right?

Even the arrangements that would be his went over his head a little. The second had a summerhouse that could be easily converted, the third an extension annexe that could just be bricked off inside to separate it from the main house. But they were just…spaces. Roofs, walls, bike spots. As long as Chris had room for his stuff and keys to the main house so he could come and go as much as Gabriel would, what did he care if the summerhouse could only be accessed by walking through the garage, or if the adjoining annexe was, in Aled's words, ugly as a pig's tits?

He was starting to have doubts about this plan.

Then the fourth place changed his mind.

It was slightly outside St Ives. A farm must have been sold off and the buildings partitioned into their own plots—a farmhouse loomed just over the hedge, and they passed a barn conversion by the road—yet the gate and gravel drive led to two stone bungalows on either side of a small, open yard. They'd plainly been built together, and the layouts were identical. Both had kitchens and bathrooms at one end, a small bedroom at the other, and an open-plan area between that was a living room, dining room and study rolled into one. The master bedroom in each was in the roof space via spiral stairs in a hidden niche that Chris had assumed to be a linen cupboard between the kitchen and the bathroom.

"We're selling them as one property because of the cellar," the agent said.

"The cellar?"

"You'll see."

The cellar stairs were accessed via the kitchen, like an old-fashioned pantry. And when they got down into the empty space, Chris did indeed see.

Specifically, he saw the matching set of stairs at the other end of the cavernous cellar, snaking up into what had to be the opposite bungalow.

"Can guess what you'd use this for," he muttered to Aled.

Aled just smirked and said nothing.

But afterwards, when they were sat in the car and the agent had locked up and left, Aled said, "That's it. That's the one."

Chris hummed.

"What're you thinking?" Aled asked.

That it felt more equal, two bungalows instead of a granny annexe behind a big house. That it would be a great cycle into the town, especially on summer mornings. That he could get that dog he'd been thinking of, with loads of room to run about. That he could be social and antisocial at the same time, with only a handful of nearby neighbours but his boyfriend and his boyfriend's boyfriend within laughably easy reach.

"It's nice," he said.

Aled chuckled. "Nice."

"Better get mine sold."

"Ah, I see," Aled said, and started the engine. "It's *nice.*"

Chapter Thirteen

They stayed Saturday night as well.

Aled had intended to take the time to talk options with Chris and negotiate at least a top two, and let Gabriel cast the deciding vote. But, as it was pretty clear which one they both wanted, he simply emailed the agent with a suitable offer, and they sat back with a pint each in the hotel bar.

"To moving."

Chris raised his glass, but frowned.

"Think Gabriel will like it?" he asked.

"How much did you tick off?"

"All the reds, all but one of the oranges and some of the greens."

"Which orange was missing?"

"No security lights," Chris said, "but I can fit those myself. I did Mum's."

"There you go, then," Aled said. "If it ticks the boxes, he'll be happy. He's pretty easy-going. Guess being homeless puts a different perspective on things."

It had actually been a pain in the backside while trying to find a new house. Aled had expected Gabriel to be as demanding about the perfect house as he was about sex. Instead he'd been so passive and agreeable that he'd agreed to every single viewing. There was a reason Aled had wanted Chris on side with a new house first.

"I suppose," Chris said. "I'm still a bit surprised he didn't want to come, though."

"He did, but the gym's short-staffed at the minute and he's raking in the overtime. There's a bug going round."

"Ah."

"Colours aside, it's ideal for his coming and going," Aled said. "He'll like being able to just flit between us."

"So will I," Chris admitted. "I've missed him since he got back on his feet. You too, to be honest."

Aled raised his glass, and Chris clanked his against it.

"Be odd to live down here," Aled admitted. "Nice, mind, but odd."

"You've never left Yorkshire?"

"Never lived outside of it, no. Hell, never even lived outside *West* Yorkshire. Cornwall's a foreign country."

"Remember to get your vaccines and bring your passport."

Aled chortled.

"You'll get used to it," Chris said. "Just remember the right way to do scones."

"It's the *South*," Aled grumbled.

Chris smirked. "Yeah, but it's not posh South."

"Says you, Somerset-boy."

Chris flipped him off. Aled snorted. He enjoyed the progress they'd made. This time last year, Chris had been too damn scared to stand in the same room as him.

"What you going to do for work?" Aled asked.

Chris shrugged. "I'll find something. Done all sorts."

Aled envied his relaxation. "That'd have me up at night."

Chris just shrugged again. "Always the dole and the army reserves. There's always *something*. What's Gabriel going to do?"

"Probably end up manning a reception desk in one of Tom's hotels. Suze is scouting out some suitable arrangements for him. Long as there's no alcohol around, he's not fussed. Though I think he'd like to find another gym job or something like it. He likes where he is now."

Chris wrinkled his nose. "Urgh. Gyms. Not for me."

"Urgh. Running. Not for me."

"Lazy."

"Fitness freak."

The waitress interrupted by delivering their food then, when she retreated, Chris raised a surprising question.

"Will you need to make a—a room? For you and him? Like Kevin does? I mean, I was kind of kidding about the cellar but…is that really what you'll need to do with it?"

"Make it into a playroom?"

"Yeah."

"Could do," Aled said, but the phrasing nagged at him. "Why would we *need* to?"

"Well, no more Kevin."

"Less Kevin," Aled corrected. "Gabriel has new rules. Visits every six weeks or so."

"Oh, right."

Aled eyed him, wondering whether Chris needed to talk something out. He could need coaxing if that were the case. But, to his surprise, Chris opened the issue without further prompting.

"Guess I'm a bit...I don't know. Worried he won't be getting what he needs once Kevin's a few hundred miles away."

"Ah."

"He's not pressured me or anything, but...you know."

"Yeah," Aled agreed. "But I wouldn't worry about it. He'll want to meet other men for a bit. Find some playthings of his own. Scout out the territory. If he's feeling a gap, he'll find someone to fill it. Always has."

"Like he does with Greg?"

Aled made a so-so gesture. "Sort of. Greg's a social thing as much as a sex thing. I can't stand those bloody gigs they go to, and Kevin's not available in the evenings thanks to having a horde of children. The sex isn't anything special, from what I gather."

"Well, Kevin, then."

"Yeah, I guess like that."

"What gap do you fill?"

"Sexually? None, really," Aled said. "I'm a bit more suitable for certain things, but he could still get those things from Kevin if he really wanted to, I suppose. What gap are you getting at?"

Chris coughed. "Erm."

Aled waited.

"Well, uh. Was — um..."

"Spit it out."

"Er—do you always—" Chris glanced around, but they were alone in their little corner. Still, he lowered his voice. "Do you always top?"

That's it?

"Yeah," Aled replied.

"You ever tried it the other way?"

"Not with him. Already knew it didn't do anything for me before I met him, and he's never asked to shake it up. Why? You curious?"

Chris went red, but cleared his throat and answered anyway.

"I guess. Wondering if—you know. Might like it better."

Aled rather suspected Chris had never had his prostate nailed.

"Fair enough," he said. "I know Gabriel used to top with one of his former playthings. Won't say boyfriend, seeing as how it was over once Jason found a steady partner."

"Why, er…"

Aled took a leisurely sip of his pint, waiting out the flustered attempts at questions.

"So, um, why don't you like it?"

"I don't *not* like it," Aled said. "Just doesn't get me going like a good game does. Feels bloody amazing, don't get me wrong, but it's just physical. And if I'm going to the effort of having sex with someone else, I'm not all that interested in it only getting me off physically."

He liked the mind games as much—if not more— than Gabriel did. He liked to *play*. To hunt. There was as much of a mental pleasure in sex with someone else as a physical one. If Aled just needed to get laid, he could have a wank. Why bother going to the effort of bottoming for someone when a quick ten minutes into his own hand would have the same result?

But Chris hummed. Plainly unconvinced, he sat rolling his half-empty glass absently between his palms.

"I just wonder if it'll do more for me than just..." He made a wanking motion, and Aled snorted with laughter.

"Only one way to find out," he said. "Least you know Gabriel isn't going to mind if you try it out and you're not bothered."

"Yeah."

Aled watched the cogs turn. He was well aware how carefully Chris overthought everything—he'd only recently come to terms with being asexual—and it didn't surprise him that Chris wanted to pick and niggle at this latest development.

But at the same time, Aled couldn't really relate. He'd figured out he was bisexual and come to terms with it in about five minutes flat. All of Chris' anxiety was centred on such ordinary, normal, vanilla stuff. Aled felt *sorry* for him. *Something* about his background had to be telling him to carry this odd shame, right?

"You worried?" he asked quietly.

Chris flashed him a brief smile.

"Not as much as I would have been this time last year," he admitted.

"That's good."

"I'm getting there."

Aled grinned as a thought—and a memory—occurred to him.

"Kind of proves Gabriel's crazy about you, you know."

"Why?"

"He's not exactly friendly about people who want to use him to experiment. I remember when we were first seeing each other, some hookup left him money and he blew his lid. Used the cash to get a taxi to mine — all the way from Leeds — for a proper fuck from a real man, as he put it."

Chris snorted with laughter. "Oh, God, yeah. He told me about that once."

"You're a definite exception," Aled said. "No way he'd have been up for any experimenting if you were somebody else. *Anybody* else."

Chris pinked, ducking his head.

"You know he was only willing to move on the condition you were coming too?" Aled murmured, sensing a soft spot.

"He, er. Yeah. He dropped a hint but I figured he was just trying to twist my arm."

"Nope. Said loud and clear he wasn't moving down south to still have to get on a train to see you," Aled said. "Guess we all know where you stand."

Chris raised his glass. Aled touched his own to it.

"To monogamous guys in polygamous relationships," Chris said.

"Polyamorous."

"What's the difference?"

Aled chuckled. "I've learned my lesson, that's the difference. I got divorced once. And I'm not daft enough to get married again."

"You gave him that charm around his neck," Chris said. "You as good as married him."

"He knows what I feel for him. That's enough. The rest of it — " Aled waved a hand. "It's an excuse to get lazy."

"You still think you would?"

"I would," Aled said. "And I'm not risking it. All of this — if he'd said no, if he'd said he wanted to stay in Yorkshire, then I'd have stayed."

"You'd have chosen him over your family?"

"Ultimately, yes."

Even saying it out loud caused a twinge in his chest. It was a horrible choice. One he'd never wanted to make and, thank God, hadn't needed to.

But ultimately, it was true. He'd tried to deny it, but it was still true. And it was the same one he'd encouraged Suze to make when she'd agonised about marrying Tom and moving away. Family could endure the distance. They would be family no matter what. There was no real risk there. But love couldn't always tolerate the same, and opening up that gap between himself and Gabriel would never have been worth the risk.

"I'd choose him over anyone," Aled said.

Chris just nodded, and they raised a toast to Gabriel.

The cornerstone of both their lives, and the biggest thing they had in common.

Chapter Fourteen

Gabriel had lied.

Sort of. He *had* been scheduled to work the weekend that Aled and Chris picked for house-shopping, but he'd wriggled out of it and swapped for the next one instead once he discovered Aled would be out of the house for the whole weekend.

And the reason why was already there when he coasted the bike into their street on Friday afternoon.

Kevin's Kit ens and Bat rooms took up Aled's usual parking spot, and while the van was locked up tight, the front door of their house gaped open and tools littered the hall. Dust coated the front garden and a saw whirred deep inside the house.

One of Kevin's rules, after all, was that he always had a key to Gabriel's home.

Once, it had been about making sure he was safe and not drinking himself into oblivion. There'd been evenings — long ago, now — where Kevin letting himself in had been the only thing standing between Gabriel and the bottle, or Gabriel and much worse than a drink. There were nights Kevin had sat up with him until dawn, just *being* there, just to stop the demons in Gabriel's head.

But for nearly six years now, Kevin had only let himself in when Gabriel had fucked up and failed to get in touch, or when he'd been invited over in the first place.

And yes, Gabriel had invited him to help put down the new laminate in the kitchen. But with Aled out of town, he was hoping to borrow Kevin for just a little bit more, too.

"Hey!" he chirped, rapping his knuckles on the kitchen doorframe and sticking his head into the room to grin at the enormous tradesman on his hands and knees in the corner. "Do you want a cup of tea?"

"Already got one," Kevin grunted around the pencil clenched between his teeth. "Fuck off and let me work."

"Need anything else?"

"You to fuck off."

"Okay, okay..."

Gabriel did a little tidying of the scattered tools, and rinsed off the plants in the front garden with the hose, but then beat a retreat and went for a shower and to don some scruffy clothes. If Kevin was going to be an antisocial grump until he was finished laying the new floor, Gabriel might as well get some of the other chores done.

By the time the sawing and hammering stopped, the bathroom was spotless, the bedsheets were changed in both the master and the spare, and he'd managed to just about — with a lot of swearing — hang the spare room door again. Once Kevin started whistling, Gabriel headed downstairs and made another brew, admiring the new floor while Kevin fiddled around with the skirting boards.

"It looks much nicer," he said. "When did you even get here?"

"About half two. Judith's taken the kids to her mum's for the day, so I ferried them all over there and then headed down."

"Well, thanks for coming," Gabriel said, then made a pass at him. "How much do I owe you?"

To his surprise, Kevin sat back on his heels and chuckled, shaking his head.

"I don't think so, angel. Last time I saw you, you were crying in my lap."

Gabriel blew upwards into his hair.

"That wasn't the *last* time," he objected. "The *last* time was when you dropped me back off at home, after dinner with you and Judith and the kids, *after* I cried in your lap."

"Same difference. How have you been?"

"Fine," Gabriel said, and softened. "Honestly. I've been fine. It must have just been the relaxant."

They didn't drug play often. In fact, Kevin was the only person he'd do any drug play with whatsoever, and the drug in question was nothing more than a muscle relaxant. It wasn't designed to interfere with his thoughts or his decision-making. Just make him less physically able to put up a fight.

"I double checked it. Nothing's changed."

"I've never spaced on it before, though," Gabriel said. "I think that's what happened. I was fine — *more* than fine — before I spaced. And then it went wrong."

"I'm nixing it then," Kevin said. "If you can't space on it without a panic attack, it's not for use anymore."

"Okay," Gabriel said. "You'll just have to keep me pliant the traditional way."

Kevin smirked, but didn't take the bait.

"I'm really all right," Gabriel coaxed.

"You had sex since?"

"Yes."

"With Aled?"

"Yes. Wednesday night." Gabriel raised his hands and did air quotes. "He 'caught me cheating' and locked me in our bedroom to remind me who I belong to."

Kevin chuckled, and the hands-off vibe thawed a little. "Did it work?"

"Define 'work'."

"Are you still cheating?"

Gabriel licked his lips. "I mean...he's away all weekend."

"*Is* he now..."

"Yeah. It gets a little lonely when he's gone. That's not my fault."

Kevin snorted, packing his tools back into his kit. "Well, there's your floor anyway. I'd get a hoover on it to get the dust off, soon as you can, then a mop."

"I can do that while you clear up," Gabriel said brightly.

"Sure. You paying with cash or card?"

Gabriel bit back the smirk. Kevin had offered to do it for free. Clearly their little sex chat had laid a few worries to rest.

But he said nothing, just, "Card."

"I'll get the machine."

Kevin loped out to the van, and Gabriel fetched the vacuum cleaner and started running the tap for a bucket and mop. The floor was a nice pale wood effect, almost white, and it brightened up the little kitchen enormously. Once he'd run the vacuum over it to snaffle up the shavings and dust, it looked a million dollars.

"Go cheap clearance sales and tradesmen for friends," he muttered to himself.

The van doors slammed just as he'd finished mopping, and Kevin shut the front door behind him too. Gabriel smirked to himself. He was *definitely* about to get some. He was already starting to ache — and with Kevin's dick, he'd been downright sore by the end of the day.

"Looks nice," Kevin said, appearing in the open doorway with his arms folded over his chest.

"It does! You've done a great job. Thank you." He put the mop back in the bucket, then feigned surprise. "You didn't get your card machine."

"I figured we could do without the bank taking their cut."

"I haven't got any cash," Gabriel apologised.

"Was thinking we could come to a different sort of agreement," Kevin drawled.

He reached out. Thick fingers caught in Gabriel's hair. The kiss was brutal — a hard smash against his mouth — and when he gasped, a hot tongue stole his air. Kevin's other hand went straight for Gabriel's jeans, squeezing his arse through the denim before beginning to pull them down. Gabriel lashed out, only for Kevin to catch both his wrists and laugh at him.

"Might as well give your boyfriend something to *really* beat you for, right? Here. I'll leave him a clue."

Teeth sank into his neck. Gabriel gasped, groaning, as heat flooded his body. He was hard in an instant. All the fight drained out of him with the rush of arousal, and he sagged in Kevin's grip like he'd been paralysed.

Then the bite eased into a gentle suck, and he recovered a few of his wits.

"L-let go of me!"

The laugh in his ear was low and filthy, then Kevin's hands closed around his throat. Gabriel stiffened. Even with Kevin, breathplay was minimal. He clawed at Kevin's wrists as the burn spread through his lungs, as the spots started to dance, as the kitchen tipped—

Wet floor.

Gabriel was dropped like a sack of rocks, and he gasped for air on the wet floor, drunk on the air and dizzy with relief. His limbs shook as Kevin turned him over and ripped his jeans down to his knees. By the time Gabriel registered the hand soap, it was far too late to do anything about it.

"No!"

Kevin's hands sealed over his mouth, Kevin's body weighed his own down like a ton of bricks, and a hard, slick dick began to push.

Gabriel screamed.

Screamed.

He opened his lungs and *howled*. Pain crackled up his spine. For a brief moment, his idiotic body fought it—then his submissive streak took over and he collapsed under Kevin's frame as, inch by inch, that truncheon of a cock forced its way into his arse.

It. Fucking. *Hurt.*

His entire being zeroed in on the pain. He didn't fight it. Didn't struggle. He simply lay there and accepted it, sobbing as it reached its peak and shuddering in a mixture of relief and horror when

Kevin slid a hand under his hips and began to lazily jack him off.

"Just relax," Kevin said. "It'll be over soon."

Gabriel blinked at the shimmering floor, dancing on the edge of subspace as Kevin began to thrust in long, idle strokes. The movement rippled up his body as though Gabriel were a calm sea disturbed by a tide. He could feel every inch, every vein, every contour. Kevin's breath was hot on the back of his neck. Huge hands held his arms down to the floor and, every now and then, Kevin would jerk Gabriel's consciousness back to his body by biting him, leaving deep bruises for Aled to find when he came home on Monday night.

When Gabriel came, it was with a wrenching sensation as if being torn free from his body.

"There you go," Kevin murmured, licking the shell of his ear as he fucked the cum right back out of Gabriel's battered body. "See? It only hurts if silly sluts like you put up a fight."

"N-no…"

"No, what? No, it's not hurting? Or no, you're not a slut?"

"Not — not a slut."

"Oh, but you *are*."

Gabriel sobbed when Kevin sat back on his heels and pulled Gabriel to his knees. The thrusts turned to sharp, short bursts of frenetic activity — hard and painful and so, so good — and, of course, the position made him gape wide open. When Kevin finally came, it flooded back out in a rush when he pulled his softening cock out, and Gabriel cringed at the feeling of blood and cum leaking down his thighs.

He cringed even harder when Kevin took a photo.

"Like the floor?"

"Y-yes."

"Held up nice, didn't it?"

"Yes."

Kevin smacked his arse. "Figured I'd give your boyfriend something to really beat you for. Say thank you."

Gabriel shook his head and received another sharp smack.

"Say *thank you*, you ungrateful little bitch."

"F-for what? You r —"

"You begged me to fuck you and keep you company while your boyfriend's out of town," Kevin snarled. "Say it!"

"No!"

Gabriel was dragged backwards by the hair until he scrambled to his knees. Kevin loomed over him, and the slap in the face was harsher than either of the blows to his backside.

"*Say it.*"

"Please go," Gabriel sobbed. "Please go, please, *please —*"

He hoped Kevin would refuse.

And the sick grin that spread over Kevin's face made his heart jump.

"Go?" he said. "You owe me a lot more than just a quick fuck on the kitchen floor. That wasn't payment. That was testing the product."

"I've paid plenty!" Gabriel spat. "You need to go. Just *go.*"

Kevin laughed. It was a cold, cruel laugh that *did* things, and it pinned Gabriel in place more effectively than any weight. He was powerless to stop it when Kevin's hands clamped down around his wrists and he was dragged out of the kitchen to the bottom of the stairs.

"Saturday rates," Kevin drawled, dropping Gabriel by the stairs and holding him down by a heavy boot in the middle of his back. The sound of metal clinking in his toolbox was delicious and terrifying at the same time.

"Please go," Gabriel begged. "I won't tell anyone. Please, please, just go."

"You're not going to be squealing," Kevin said. "The way you were coming on to me? The way your boyfriend beats you for being a whore? Nah. You won't be saying a thing."

The rope bit into Gabriel's wrists like tiny teeth, and his wrists were tied to the banister with deft, skilled hands. He knew from years of experience that Kevin's knots would never give way in a million years, but he yanked anyway, stilling only when Kevin cupped his chin between finger and thumb and looked him dead in the eye.

"I'm going to make use of your shower," he murmured. "And then maybe your washing machine. Clean off these scruffy overalls. And while they're drying on your nice warm radiators, I think you can offer me a good Saturday rate as well. How does that sound?"

Gabriel spat in his face.

The blow was deafening. The room spun. Blood burst into his mouth and bubbled over his lips — and then Kevin pinched his chin again, and held his gaze once more.

"Do that again," he whispered, "and your boyfriend will come home to scrub your blood out of that nice new floor. Got it?"

Gabriel nodded.

"Good."

Kevin patted his cheek, straightened up and stomped away upstairs.

Leaving Gabriel with a bloody lip, aching wrists, and a hard-on that refused to be ignored.

Chapter Fifteen

It was just after midday when Aled pulled up outside Chris' house.

"So…what now?" Chris asked.

"Er. You get out?"

Chris snorted. "I mean about the house."

"Get yours up for sale," Aled said. "Don't accept any offer less than the two-twenty she quoted you as a mid-range."

"What about the deposit?"

"I can handle that."

The idea of Aled having so much just lying around in savings was scary enough to let Chris pop open the door.

"Just stay in touch," Aled said. "It's not as stressful as folks make out."

"Sure," Chris said sceptically.

He watched Aled pull away, then turned to let himself in through the gate. Curtains were twitching at the neighbours' windows. No doubt more whispering about Karen's odd'un gallivanting off with strange men in flash cars. At least they were probably assuming he was involved in drug dealing rather than having boyfriends. He shrugged it off as he let himself into the bungalow, stooping to stroke Noodle as the cat swished past and escaped.

"Hello to you too," he muttered.

He topped up the food bowls, changed the litter tray and threw his clothes in the wash before showering and finding fresh ones. His hair was starting to go fluffy, so he shaved it along with his jaw before flopping down on his bed and firing off a text.

Me: Aled's on his way home to you. Just dropped me off.

He'd long since given up on figuring out Gabriel's work pattern, but was still surprised by the speed of the reply.

Gabriel: Is it true you've put an offer in?

Chris: How do you know that already?

Gabriel: He texted me this morning.

Gabriel: Duh.

Gabriel: But was he being serious?

Gabriel: Have you really actually chosen one?

Chris raised his eyebrows, not sure which route to go down first. Eventually, he decided Gabriel was glued to his phone fairly often and ignored the speed. He probably hadn't been waiting with bated breath for updates. And he supposed it wasn't too surprising that Aled had already been in touch, seeing as how he wouldn't be able to for most of the long drive north. But the shock they'd picked somewhere was a bit rude. That had been the point, hadn't it?

Me: Why so surprised?

Gabriel: Because that man can't make a decision for the life of him so it must be your fault!

Chris smirked.

Me: Not guilty. It was a joint effort.

Gabriel: BS!

Me: Nope. God's honest truth. We both liked it. And I ticked off most of your traffic light list. We think you'll like it too.

Gabriel: You'd better have ticked them off if you're BUYING it!

Gabriel: So which one was it?

Gabriel: You got all my must-haves, right?

Gabriel: Right???

Me: Yes. And the last one. Out in the country.

Gabriel: Ooh, the rural bungalows?

Gabriel: You and Aled just across the garden from each other? And me wherever I like?

Gabriel: Good cycling country?

Me: Yes, yes, and looks it but I didn't take my bike so haven't tested it.

Gabriel: Yesssss xxx

Gabriel: Maybe if I bribe Aled with sex at Land's End, we can finally get him on a bike.

Me: Good luck with that. If it didn't work in the Dales it's not going to work in Cornwall…

Gabriel sent him a grumpy emoji, and Chris grinned before leaving him to his plotting. No amount of sex would get Aled on a bike. He hated them. In fact, now Gabriel would have permanent company on his jaunts, Chris was pretty sure Aled would stop agreeing to ferry the bikes around too. Two of them could handle any trouble that came their way, so why should Aled have to be backup anymore? That would be his logic.

Chris abandoned the texting to ring the estate agent and book an appointment for the following week, then texted it to Aled and heaved himself up off the bed when another joke thrown Gabriel's way got no reply. He might as well make himself some lunch, then have a kip and recharge from all the socialising.

He was tired and a little drained from having to be sociable all weekend, and he'd intended to get his head down for a few hours once Aled was gone. He had work tomorrow, which meant customers and being pleasant and all that exhausting crap. He needed to recover. But something pulled him towards the garden instead of the kitchen, and he let himself out of the back door into the wilderness.

If there was one thing that he and Mum had managed to understand about each other over the years, it was a love of the outdoors. She'd never had much money and they'd lived off her meagre wages, dried corned beef sandwiches and whatever spare change could be squeezed from his grandparents' pensions. Once his uncle had been dishonourably discharged for that incident with the sheep, his contribution to keeping his sister and nephews fed and clothed had dried up too. And because they lived in a country village, not an inner city sink estate, there'd been next to nothing in the way of help from the government.

So Mum's way of keeping them busy and entertained had been anything that was free. And walking across the levels, exploring hidden caves in the Mendips, following rivers to the sea or their source, had all been free. Chris had grown up rambling around the countryside, collecting leaves for art projects at home, kicking a football about with just his mum and his brother in the middle of nowhere, climbing trees on his own instead of getting to go to the birthday parties at the adventure centre near Bristol.

Tim had never been all that bothered, but it had given Chris a love of nature and the outdoors that had been a refuge over the years. And if Mum hadn't understood what he was hiding from or why, she'd at least understood why the refuge was what it was.

The garden showed it best of all. She'd never kept a trim lawn and tidy borders — and Chris hadn't exactly kept on top of the gardening since she'd died.

Flowering shrubs jostled for room. A vegetable patch at the back was duelling with a persistent crop of brambles. Weeds thrived merrily amongst the wanted plants, and the remains of a wasps' nest glowered warningly from the eaves of the rotting shed. The gravel that ran along the back fence was almost completely obscured by moss, and the little stone angel tucked into a corner was spotted with bird shit again.

Chris slid down the fence to sit with the angel and looked back at the bungalow through heavy eyes.

"Guess neither of you would've seen this coming, huh?"

Mum had bought the angel to serve as a grave marker of sorts after they'd scattered Tim's ashes in the garden. Chris had scattered hers at the exact same spot. And though he didn't really believe they could hear him or they existed in some other reality or level of existence, he'd always found a little comfort in coming out into the garden. First to talk to Tim, and now to talk to Mum, too.

God knew he hadn't been able to talk to them when they'd been alive.

"I'm moving away," he told the angel. "I'm selling the house and I'm moving to Cornwall. I'm going to start somewhere new."

Somewhere that he could be himself.

"I'm going with my boyfriend. And his boyfriend."

Saying the words out loud—here in Mum's garden, next to Tim's angel—was followed by a dizzy rush. Something snapped in his chest. A weight across the back of his neck eased.

"You'd both hate Gabriel," he said. "He's gay. Acts it, looks it, *is* it. And poly. He loves both me *and* Aled, and he has this other guy who's like family to him as well, and he still has random hookups every now and then because he likes trying out sex with new people occasionally. You'd think he's a real freak."

Mum wouldn't say it out loud, but Tim would have. Even if he'd worked past the whole Chris-was-with-a-dude thing. He'd probably have tried to go and thump Gabriel or something.

"He's trans, too. And he wouldn't care if you hated that. He'd laugh in your faces and say he was living a better life than you were. You know, sometimes he says I need to learn that trick."

He took a deep breath and ripped the plaster off the wound.

"I know you were both ashamed of me."

A breeze rippled through the garden, shaking shrub leaves and disturbing a few enterprising bees from their tasks. One landed briefly on Chris' hand before righting itself and zipping away again.

Just weather, but somehow it felt like a denial.

"I *know* you were," Chris said. "And so was I. For the longest time. But now — "

Now he was moving in with a partner and his partner's partner, and he didn't care about what it looked like. He wasn't afraid of Aled like he had been in the past. He'd shaken off the family wisdom that a gay relationship was inferior, that polyamory was cheating, that there was any happiness or permanence in relationships that weren't like theirs had always been.

He leaned back against the fence and smiled at the sparrows watching him suspiciously from the roof.

"I'm starting over where I'm just me. Just Chris. Not your weird kid or weird brother. And if people figure out I have a boyfriend, good for them. I can take 'em.

And if people think I'm gay, then whatever. I'm not going to worry about it anymore."

Maybe he hadn't figured out all the sex stuff yet, and maybe he'd experiment a little bit more in the future, and maybe he wouldn't. Maybe he'd get used to saying he was asexual. Maybe he'd figure out what the hell his romantic orientation was supposed to be. Maybe, maybe, maybe.

And maybe he wouldn't.

"It doesn't matter like I thought it did."

Chapter Sixteen

It was half-past-six on Sunday before Aled got home.

He couldn't remember if Gabriel was working that afternoon or not, and the text he'd sent from the motorway services when he'd stopped for a leak had gone unanswered. But he pulled up outside the house just in time to see the lights go on upstairs, and figured that he'd either catch Gabriel in his cycling gear and heading for the shower, or with another man.

He was wrong on both counts.

He let himself in to find tools all over the hall floor, a freshly painted and rehung living room door, and the smell of sawdust permeating everything. The banisters had been sanded down and repainted, and a bucket of dirty water by the radiator said it had finally been bled.

Upstairs, the bathroom door closed.

Aled tossed out the filthy water then locked the front door and headed up, shedding his outer layers on the way. Gabriel was singing when Aled rapped his knuckles on the bathroom door, and it stopped instantly.

"I'm ho-ome," Aled called through the wood.

The door was flung open, and a messy mixture of paint, dust and human being threw its arms around his neck.

"Hello," Aled said, laughing at the exuberance. "Been busy?"

"The boiler failed at work so they're closed until tomorrow when the engineer can come out," Gabriel explained. "Good trip? Successful? Are we buying a house?"

"Yes, yes and yes," Aled said, ruffling Gabriel's hair. It was greyer than an old man's, and he raised his eyebrows at the battered face. "What happened to you?"

"Kevin."

"Ahh. Have fun?"

"Yep. Then came home and finished up a few chores."

"Hence the dust?"

"Hence the dust."

"You need a wash."

"So do you. You smell like a petrol station and that shitty air freshener."

"You smell like a B&Q store."

"Better than your shitty air freshener. Care to join me?"

Aled never passed on an offer to share the shower, even if he had no real urge to fuck. Naked, wet Gabriel might change his dick's mind. And even if he stayed switched off, the view would still be better than the tiles on his own.

"You'll be pleased to know the place we've picked has an over-the-bath shower instead of a cubicle," he said, herding Gabriel back into the bathroom and shutting the door behind them. "You can have one of your post-game soaks in the tub again."

"Thank God," Gabriel said. "Which reminds me. Before you freak out, this was an accident."

He turned his back and wriggled out of his grubby T-shirt. Aled didn't have to ask what he meant. Several savage stripes criss-crossed his back — telltale signs of a whipping — and one was held together by a row of neat black stitches.

"What happened?" Aled asked, tracing it gently with his thumb.

"You'll laugh."

"Go on, then…"

"So Kevin picked me up from work on Friday for some fun and games because Judith's taken the kids to see their nan for the weekend, and you know how Kevin and his in-laws get on…"

"Uh-huh."

"So we're playing this slave-training game, and I wanted a really good, deep, *savage* fuck, so I wasn't behaving and Kevin decides to beat me. So he gets me tied up and face-down over the coffee table and he's going away at my back and it's one of those where he won't stop until I safeword, so I'm trying to draw it out as long as possible…"

Aled winced. He wasn't a fan of getting *that* brutal. He leaned forward and kissed one of the pink welts before cupping Gabriel's neck in both hands and starting a massage.

"*Fuck*, that's nice…"

"So what happened? Not like Kevin to miss."

"Turns out last week they finally bought a kitten for the girls."

"Oh my God…"

"And we usually play in the workshop so of course I wasn't exactly expecting a hairy *thing* to attack my hair."

Aled chuckled. "Oh Christ, I can see where this is going."

"So I lurch up screaming, thinking there's a rat hanging off my head, and *wham*. Belt comes down and the buckle splits me open from top to toe and there's blood *everywhere* and Kevin's calling for red and I'm just like, 'Get this fucking vermin off my fucking face!' because I've got a blindfold on and I can't see for shit and then he's like, 'It's just a kitten. What the hell did you think it was?' And then it runs off under the sofa and Kevin's saying I need to go to hospital because he's ripped a strip off me, and all I'm thinking is I never got my orgasm."

"Trust you," Aled remarked. "And this is *not* Kevin's handiwork. What did you tell the A&E staff?"

"The truth," Gabriel said chirpily. "The doctor wanted to sink through the floor and die. Or maybe call the cops, not sure."

"I'll bet," Aled said, smirking. "I take it you shut the kitten out after that?"

"Well, Kevin just took me home and fucked me regular, but I guess so. Once it's healed and I can goad him into beating me again."

"Think that's going to be a scar before you'll manage that," Aled said.

"Nah, he'll just be more creative until it's ready."

"When most people say creative, they mean painting or writing poetry. Not how to torture someone without causing more damage from the *last* time you tortured someone."

Gabriel just rolled his head back into Aled's palms and grinned up at him. "I'm not most people."

"Clearly," Aled drawled, then kissed him between the eyes. "Get in that shower then, and I'll give you a proper back massage."

"Ooh, yes please."

Aled had learned quite a few massage techniques after Gabriel's car accident, to help with the vertigo and depression. And it paid off in spades when he sank his thumbs into Gabriel's shoulder blade and watched the knot pop and dissipate as Gabriel groaned like a porn star. He worked under the hot water until all the stiffness had been eradicated, then—rather than reaching for the shower gel and scrubbing—Gabriel simply turned around, looped his arms around Aled's neck, and kissed him.

They had had vanilla sex perhaps four or five times in their entire relationship. But up against the tiles and with miles of hot, wet skin to explore, Aled couldn't be bothered turning it into a game. He sank to his knees and blew Gabriel as slowly and tantalisingly as possible, and only reached for the soap when it was over.

"Thanks," Gabriel mumbled, resting his head against Aled's shoulder as Aled washed the muck out of that inky hair. "M't go to sleep now."

"No dinner?"

"Feed me tomorrow."

Aled chuckled, kissing his forehead. "Yeah, well, stay awake long enough to get into bed, okay?"

"No pr'mises…"

Sure enough, he catnapped pretty much immediately after getting dried off and tipped into bed, but Aled wasn't bothered. Gabriel had developed a habit of power naps during his recovery and hadn't really shaken it. By the time Aled had puttered about with the vacuum cleaner and tidied up the remnants of DIY and house painting, Gabriel had burrowed into the duvet, woken up a bit and put a film on.

"Come on," he said, patting Aled's side of the bed when Aled checked in on him. "Come hug me. And tell me about our new house!"

Aled turned the volume down and did as he was told, sliding into the bed and immediately ending up with a lapful.

"Sure you want us to put an offer in without you seeing it?"

"Show me which one it was out of the options."

Aled called up the list on his phone. Gabriel had gone through with him to help choose some likely candidates, but he'd not been all that specific about what he was after until he wrote his list. He'd certainly never mentioned a favourite option.

"There."

"Ooh, the one in the country. I thought you wanted to be closer?"

"To be honest, I fell a bit in love," Aled admitted. "And Chris was keen as well."

"So make me fall in love."

"It's private, Chris and I will take a bungalow each and you can spread yourself out across both, there's a nice spot in the yard for your hammock and there's space for a playroom."

Gabriel's ears pricked up. "A playroom?"

"Yup. Big cellar underneath with stairs up into both bungalows."

"Ooh."

"We can put up a dividing wall if Chris wants some storage space, or leave it open."

"He's not exactly going to want to join us."

Aled decided to keep their anal sex discussion to himself and moved swiftly on.

"Only thing missing is a garage. If we make enough profit from this place, we could have one built. Or we could just buy a shed for the bikes and call it a day."

"It's proper in the country, then?"

"Yep. Road outside turns into a single dirt track after another couple of hundred yards."

"Wow," Gabriel breathed. "I'm going to live in the country."

"Big dream of yours?" Aled asked.

"Not really. I never *dared* to dream about it," Gabriel admitted. He took Aled's phone and started swiping through the pictures. "I mean, when I still wanted to shag everything that moved, the country would have sucked. But with you and Chris and I guess Daz again now we're going South..."

"Isn't he married now?"

"Yeah. I've fucked the husband, too. My first threesome."

Aled laughed. "All right, fair enough."

"It looks nice," Gabriel said. He swiped out of the ad and into Aled's photo album. "Oh good, you took more photos."

"Figured you'd want to explore."

They slowly slid down the bed together, Gabriel eventually wriggling sideways to lie with his head in Aled's lap as Aled channel-surfed for something more interesting and Gabriel made decorating plans. He was turning out to be more of a DIY fan than Aled had anticipated.

"All your furniture's not going to fit," Gabriel said. "We're keeping the cuddle chair but the corner sofa isn't going to work with these floor plans. And if our bedroom's that big, can we upgrade to a king size? And—"

"And we can think about it and look at our budget once we've moved."

"Oh!" Gabriel finally looked up from the phone. "I forgot to tell you. Suze called."

"She didn't text me…"

"No, she rang for *me*. She's landed me a job."

Aled grinned. "Yeah?"

"It's just maternity cover, but it's a job. I can get my foot in the door somewhere. And it ends in April, so the summer jobs for the tourists will be opening up and I can hopefully just launch right into something else."

"Doing what?"

"Admin assistant at a local legal firm. Eleven pounds an hour."

It was slightly less than he got at the gym, but he was right—a job was a job. And for all that Gabriel didn't even have so much as a GCSE to his name, he'd always done well in work. Aled supposed it wasn't too much of a stretch to hope he'd land a permanent contract if they liked him.

"In that case," he said, raking his hands through Gabriel's damp hair, "I guess we can think about that king size."

Gabriel leaned up for a kiss, then tapped Aled's nose with one finger.

"I know you've been keeping your level-headed lid on things," he whispered.

Aled blinked. "Er."

"It's okay," Gabriel said. "You can get excited if you want."

"You...sure?"

Truth be told, Aled *had* been keeping a lid on it. Much as Gabriel had never been precious about where he lived, Cornwall was a long way from the life he'd built for himself in Leeds. Aled had wanted to give him room to be nervous, even apprehensive.

But Gabriel just beamed up at him, and Aled relaxed.

"Thank you," he said, and stretched for another kiss. "It's going to be great for us. All three of us."

Gabriel followed him up for a third kiss, and as Aled was slowly drawn back into another surprisingly vanilla screw, the thought occurred that he'd better hurry up and get the house on the market.

And make Gabriel's newfound dream a reality.

Chapter Seventeen

Kevin: You busy?

Gabriel winced.

Me: Depends. Red to anything and everything sexual.

Kevin: ???

Kevin: What's wrong?

Gabriel began to type a reply, but groaned when the phone lit up and started ringing.

"I'm okay," he said upon answering it. "Don't freak out."

"You have to admit, you vetoing *anything* sexual is unusual," Kevin replied. "What's the matter?"

"Just had my smear test," Gabriel replied. "I'm walking back into town now."

"If it helps, I was thinking sexual *after* what I wanted to nick you for," Kevin said. "Got any plans today?"

"Apart from feeling sorry for myself?"

Gabriel had only gone to get his smear tests done after a blazing row with Aled a couple of years ago, when Aled found out he'd never bothered. And snitched to Kevin, who'd blown his lid. And Gabriel still felt sore about it. They didn't get it. They were cis. Any probing done in their genital areas didn't come with an added helping of dysphoria on top of the general discomfort of having a doctor's fingers where they shouldn't be.

"Apart from that," Kevin said.

"Not really."

"Good. I'm on my way. Where you at?"

"Nearly in town. What about you?"

"Just hit Outwood."

Gabriel changed course. "I'll wait outside the private school, then. You can pull in at the gate and I'll jump in. You in the work van?"

"Naw. Car today. Got the day off."

"Your ancient car that doesn't know what a mobile phone is?"

"Yeah. So?"

"So you're using the phone. While driving."

Kevin snorted. "No cops about."

"Doesn't make you *any* less of a tit," Gabriel sniped, and hung up. He pocketed the phone so as not to answer if Kevin rang again, and walked through the housing estate to get to the private school instead. Shabby houses, fancy school. Go figure.

He pulled himself up to sit on the wall and wait. The main road came whizzing by the school and he watched the traffic idly. This part of Wakefield, he definitely wouldn't miss. He'd not liked cycling around the city much *before* his accident, never mind after the fact. Nice, quiet roads and decent country air were going to be *amazing*.

He might even be able to persuade Aled to get on a bike once in a while.

Kevin drove like a moron, and his car squealed into the opening for the school gates in far too short a time to have come down from Outwood under the speed limit. Gabriel pulled a face at him, but shoved some junk off the passenger seat and got in anyway.

"You're going to get a ticket."

"Not the first time," Kevin said, jerking the wheel and pulling out in front of an angry mum. He flipped her off in the rear view.

"What's got you wound up?" Gabriel asked.

"Took today off to get some shit sorted, and wound up running around after Judith's fuckin' mum."

"Ohhh."

Kevin's mother-in-law was only better than his sister-in-law for keeping her racism to a dull roar. No wonder he was edgy.

"The answer's still red," Gabriel said. "Sorry. Try again tomorrow."

Kevin chuckled. "Don't need you for that. Check out the glovebox."

"No thanks."

"Oi! Cheeky. It's not sexual."

Gabriel opened the glovebox. A can of antifreeze fell in his lap.

"Gee, thanks."

"Not that. Put that back, though."

He did, and slid out the wad of papers. Insurance documents. The vehicle's logbook. Some *other* vehicle's logbook.

"Why do you have this?"

"Don't ask."

"All right..."

He finally found the piece of paper Kevin presumably wanted him to find, and unfolded it. A pretty black and white drawing of a chain and padlock were on it, the padlock locked and inscribed with the letter *K*.

"What's this?"

"An idea I had. Your going-away present. And a reminder. Though it's up to you."

Although Gabriel always had a choice in the form of his safewords, to have Kevin say it upfront was unusual. It typically wasn't necessary. They'd known each other too long for that.

"Well, what's the idea?"

"That you get that tattooed around your ankle. Little reminder of your owner in the North."

Gabriel hesitated. The design was gorgeous, and the idea itself appealed. But it threw up a *massive* question mark.

Kevin wasn't his only owner. And he'd never discussed tattoos with the other one.

"Aled and I have never discussed tattoos."

"Really?"

"He's not interested. And I've never had one. So...I mean, I like the idea and it's a pretty design. But I don't know if he'll like it."

"Call him and ask."

Gabriel put the paper back and found his phone again, but he was sceptical of an answer. It was half-past-ten. Aled would probably be in another one of his boring meetings.

Sure enough, the phone rang but was cancelled within seconds. So Gabriel sat back and sent a text.

Me: Call me please x

"No joy?"

"Meeting. He'll step out in a minute and call me back. I don't usually phone him."

"Don't freak the poor guy out."

"I won't! I put a kiss on it. You don't put kisses in urgent texts."

"*I* don't. You might."

"I'm not *that* inconsidera — hey, Aled."

Thankfully, Aled had taken the kiss as Gabriel meant it. He sounded perfectly calm.

"Hey. Sorry, I've just stepped out of a budget meeting. You have five minutes."

"Don't need five. Just wanted to ask, are tattoos okay in our agreement?"

They had a little black book with their BDSM and RACK boundaries in it. Mostly things that were forbidden, rather than expressing permission for other things.

"In what context?" Aled asked.

"Kevin wants to give me a tattoo to remind me of my northern owner," Gabriel explained. "Is that okay?"

"Where?"

"My ankle."

"What's the design?"

"Padlock and chain with the letter *K* on it."

"That's it?"

"Yep."

"Sure," Aled said. "If you want me to think one up for the other foot, though, you might be stretching it. Not my area."

The idea hadn't occurred to Gabriel, and he stretched out his leg in the footwell of Kevin's car, eyeing it speculatively. Kevin's padlock and chain. Maybe the first bike route he and Chris had ever done together? That had been the Trans Pennine trail from Barnsley northwards, so that could go up the back of his calf. And —

He touched the charm around his neck that Aled had given him at Tom and Suze's wedding a couple of years ago, and smiled.

And a rune on the top of his foot, for the man he'd not-quite-but-sort-of agreed to theoretically marry.

"That's okay," he said. "I have an idea or two. I'll run them by you tonight."

"You coming home tonight?"

"Yeah. It's a red day."

"Ah. Okay. See you later. Love you."

"You too," he said, and hung up.

"Good to go?" Kevin asked.

"Yup."

"I can't believe you've never talked about tattoos," Kevin remarked as they soared back towards Leeds.

"When we first got together, I said no branding or permanent marking or anything like that and that was the end of it," Gabriel said. "I never said tattoos specifically, but I guess that covered it. And he's not interested in body art, so he never asked."

"He doesn't have any?"

"Nope."

"Vanilla bastard."

Gabriel snorted with laughter. "Sure, Kevin. Whatever you say."

Kevin had a moderate amount of ink, but Judith was the tattoo gun junkie, really. Gabriel liked his piercings, but he'd never had the money for ink, nor really the inclination. They couldn't be worried the way a piercing could to create a buzz during sex, and he'd be too scared of breaking the skin and marring the tattoo through a violent game.

But his ankle would be okay. His feet never really got involved unless he was shackled to the bed. And they could just get padded cuffs for that.

Kevin's preferred parlour was in Leeds city centre, and they had to walk through the drizzle from the NCP multistorey. Thunder was brewing overhead, and the shops were busy as people sought shelter.

"What would you have done if I'd said no?" Gabriel asked as they dodged around prams and scooters.

"Got a new one for myself. Got to add Gabby's name to my list."

"You still haven't done that?"

"Been too bloody busy. After you."

Gabriel was waved into a small tattoo parlour that he recognised. He'd had his nipple pierced here. He smiled at the piercing guy, Tommy, but let Kevin guide him into the back to a woman with green hair and a *lot* of ink.

"Oh, hey, Kevin! This your boyfriend?"

"Yup."

"We doing your ankle today, hun?"

"Sure."

They played around for a while getting the positions right. Gabriel opted for his left ankle, and while Nat stencilled the design in place, he brought up a map of the Barnsley section of the Trans Pennine trail and sketched it out on a scrap piece of paper. Why not go the whole hog?

"You sure, hun?" Nat said when he asked her to add the trail and the rune. "It's gonna be a painful session for you, all these sensitive bits at once."

"I'm used to a bit of pain."

"Well, okay, sweetie."

He looked down at his foot. The Trans Pennine trail snaking its way up the side of the arch. Kevin's chain and padlock around his ankle. And Aled's charm in pride of place on the top of his foot, right over all the sensitive nerves that Gabriel liked to have stroked in the middle of a post-coital cuddle.

Oh, yeah.

This was going to *hurt*.

* * * *

Aled came to pick him up from Kevin's.

After an excruciating four hours in the tattoo parlour, Kevin had taken Gabriel home for some of Judith's special carbonara. He'd eaten in the lounge with his swollen foot up on a stool, the girls clamouring for tattoos of their own. So by the time Aled arrived from work, Gabriel was cuddling the baby on his knee while Judith patiently applied stick-on tattoos of stars and unicorns to her other two daughters. Kevin the con artist had opted to do the dishes instead.

"Hey," Aled said, appearing in the living room doorway. "You ready to get gone?"

"I don't know," Gabriel said with a grin. "Someone else needs to hold the baby."

"Not it," Aled deadpanned. "How did the tattoo go?"

"Hurt like a — like hell, but it looks great."

Aled raised his eyebrows at the crud-soaked clingfilm around Gabriel's foot.

"It'll look great when that comes off, trust me."

"When's that?"

"When we get home," Gabriel said. "And then Kevin says I should probably wear an old sock to bed, or I'll ruin the sheets."

"Wouldn't be the first time," Aled quipped. "Come on. Let's get you home."

Kevin came to take the baby, who immediately started whimpering. Gabriel decided to bail quickly, doling out rapid kisses to the other two and a hug for Judith before heading for the door.

"Call me and let me know how it is in the morning," Kevin called, bouncing his youngest in both arms. "Come on, you. What's all that for, eh? *He's* not your old man."

The whimpering dialled up into a scream, and Gabriel hastily shut the door on it, limping out to the car.

"What bit Gabby?" Aled asked.

"It's nearly dinner time," Gabriel replied, sinking into the passenger seat. "God, that's better. Hey, guess what."

"What?"

"You and Chris are on my foot too."

Aled snorted. "Right..."

"No, you are! I got the first route I ever did with Chris tattooed up the side of my foot. And then the rune you gave me at Suze's wedding on the top. And then Kevin is the padlock and chain."

Aled eyed the gunky foot.

"Show me later," he said. "When it looks decent. Or better yet, show me tomorrow."

"Why tomorrow?"

"Because you're on a red day," he replied as he started the engine, "and if you think I'm not going to want to fuck you after seeing that charm permanently inked on your skin, then you're not as clever as I thought you were."

Gabriel smirked, sinking low in his seat as they headed for home.

"Well," he said. *"Maybe* I'm on a yellow day now…"

"No dice," Aled said. "Tomorrow morning, and it won't be the foot that's making you walk funny."

Gabriel crossed his fingers and made a mental note to call in sick for work.

Chapter Eighteen

The train rattled into St Ives' tiny station, and the driver — rather pointlessly — informed them that it was the end of the line.

Thankfully, the wet weather in Somerset hadn't reached Cornwall. Chris stepped down onto a platform bathed in warm sun, and his anxiety eased a fraction. At least his CVs wouldn't get ruined before he could hand them out.

Chris hated job-hunting. It never came naturally to him — talking to strangers was something he avoided whenever possible — and the fluffy responses didn't help. Were they hiring, yes or no. Would they actually call, yes or no. He hated the dithering lack of response that most places gave.

But, not knowing anyone in St Ives, he couldn't exactly go asking his mates for work. So he squared his shoulders and set off into the town.

He'd been organised for once. He'd written three different CVs and split them into three different folders — one for retail, one for food and one for manual labour. A job was a job. He'd take whatever was going, and switch to something better once he'd settled in and gathered some contacts to let him jump ship.

Food went first—his favourite option, and the one he'd put the most effort into. Bakeries, pubs, cafes, whatever. St Ives was full of eateries, from boutique ice cream shops to independent cafes from the 1970s with chequered tablecloths. Chris dropped off nearly every CV somewhere different before he moved on to the dreaded retail folder.

By lunchtime, he'd covered most of the town and set up shop in a corner of one of the busier cafes with a local paper, circling the job ads in the back. As he'd expected, St Ives relied on a lot of seasonal work. But he imagined it would suffer from the same problem as most places—a lot of lazy Brits unwilling to do the heavy lifting. And by the ads, he was right. There were plenty of manual labour jobs going, and several local farms wanting help ready for the harvest season. He made a mental note to add getting a driving licence to his long-term plans.

Then a voice said, "Chris? Chris Wheeler?"

He jumped a mile, lurching back from the paper like it had shot him. A blonde woman with a buggy had stopped by his table, beaming over a large takeaway cup at him.

"It *is*, isn't it?" she said.

"Er," Chris said. "Yeah. Do—do I know you?"

Sweat prickled uncomfortably under his arms. He racked his brain but came up empty. He didn't know her. He was *sure* he didn't know her.

"We've never met," she said, to his enormous relief. "I'm Suze. Aled's sister."

"Oh. *Oh.*"

"I recognise you from Gabriel's Instagram," she said with a laugh. "Sorry, I didn't mean to startle you. It's nice to finally meet you face-to-face."

"You too," he said weakly.

"What are you doing here? Aled didn't mention a visit…"

"Aled's not here," he said. "Just me. Figured I'd get a head start on finding a new job."

"Oh! You're looking for work too?"

"Yeah."

"Mind if I join you?" she asked, gesturing to the empty seat.

"Er, no, go ahead…"

He did, actually. Making small talk with a stranger wasn't on his to-do list. He'd briefly met her husband, Tom, but Suze had just had a baby or had been expecting a baby or — there'd been something to do with a baby that meant she'd not been able to visit while Gabriel had been in hospital. By the time she had, Chris had gone back to Nailsea.

"What kind of work are you looking for?" she asked, settling herself with her huge coffee. The baby in the buggy was dead to the world, and Chris hoped it stayed that way.

"Anything, really. I've been CV-dropping."

"What have you done before?"

Chris shrugged. "I work at a garage at the minute. Booking appointments, invoices, that kind of thing. Done catering, house painting, worked in a bike shop…I can do whatever, really. Ex-army, so I'm a bit of a jack of all trades."

And master of none, but he didn't add that part.

"And what do you *want* to do?" she pressed.

Chris rolled his eyes. She really was Aled's sister.

"Cover my bills and keep a roof over my head," he said dryly. "I'm looking for a job, not a career."

She laughed. "You sound like my brother-in-law."

"Eh. I work to live."

"Now you *really* sound like him." She chuckled. "Okay, but—what's hell to you? What job would you instantly be looking elsewhere?"

"Customer service, I guess. I prefer the back-room type stuff."

"Can I have one of your CVs?"

"I guess."

He had a spare for manual labour, and slid it across the table to her. Her pragmatic manner was putting him at ease a little.

"This is pretty good," she said. "Would you be up for outdoors work?"

"Yeah."

"A lot of the farms like having help during the late summer when the crops come in."

"Yeah, I'm looking at them now."

"But that'll only be for a month or two."

"Better than no months."

"True." She drummed her fingers on the table, then snapped them. "Eddie."

"Er—"

"Sorry. One of my brothers-in-law. Not the one you sound like," she added. "He runs an adventure park in Hayle. He can always do with more people to help groundskeeping and with the maintenance."

"Where the hell's Hayle?"

"Just a bit farther down the coast. You could ride it. You're into cycling, right? That's how you met Gabriel?"

"Yeah."

"I'll show this to Eddie and talk you up, if you like."

"Um. That—thanks. Er."

She giggled. "Don't look so terrified!"

"I just—sorry, not really sure why you're helping me."

"You'll have to get used to that," she said briskly. "You're one of Gabriel's. And Gabriel is Aled's. And Aled's my brother, which makes us family. And we look out for family around here."

"Erm—"

"Or you can call it selfish," she continued. "If you can't find work, you might not come. And if you won't come, Gabriel won't either. And if Gabriel won't, Aled *definitely* won't and then I don't get my best friend living round the corner again like he should be. So call it selfish, if it makes you feel better."

Weirdly, it did. He could cope with that more easily than a total stranger deciding he was family and trying to find him a job.

"I'm looking for Gabriel, too," she said. "He's more the customer service type, though. And my husband owns a hotel chain, so that's not too difficult, really!"

"Do your hotels have kitchens?"

"Most of them. Why?"

Chris shrugged. "I can do kitchen work, too. I like cooking. I was training as a chef before I went into the army."

"*Really*," she said, and grinned. "Well then, I might be able to find something closer to home for you too. Give me a week. Your phone number's on here, right?"

"Yeah."

He mentally crossed his fingers. He'd only been a teenager, but the kitchen had been the best job he'd ever had. The wait staff had to deal with the actual customers, and angry chefs and cooking staff were nothing compared to knobhead squaddies. And his army-induced cool would serve well in a hot, busy environment like a restaurant or hotel kitchen.

"It wouldn't pay well," she warned. "Eddie pays his grounds staff better than we pay our kitchen skivvies."

Chris shrugged. "Doesn't matter. We're buying outright, me and Aled. And there'll be three of us working. We'll be okay."

"And no kids like this little monster," she said, shaking the buggy lightly. The baby stirred but didn't wake up. "He's gorgeous, though. Are *you* going to have any children?"

"Don't think so," he said, but his nose wrinkled of its own accord and she laughed.

"No wonder you and Aled get along."

As far as Chris knew, Aled physically couldn't have kids. And Gabriel had been making noises about having his ovaries out. So maybe soon it would only be Chris left who *could*.

But the idea didn't appeal, and he said as much.

"It's definitely a big commitment," Suze said. "But I've always wanted them. A baby brother or sister for Euan, and then I'm done."

"That's not what I've heard."

"If you've heard it from Aled, you can tell him to shut his mouth," she returned.

The baby finally stirred and began to grumble, and Suze sighed heavily, draining her coffee and abandoning the empty cardboard cup on the table.

"I'll have to go," she said. "He's been constipated lately so I don't want that shit-splosion happening here."

Chris gagged.

"I'll give you a call sometime next week," she said. "Good luck with the hunting! Let me know how it goes."

"Uh, tha—"

But she was already gone. Chris blinked, then reached for his phone.

Me: Your sister best friend whatever just accosted me in a cafe in St Ives.

Aled's reply was immediate.

Aled: Should have been more careful then, shouldn't you?

Aled: What did she want anyway?

Me: To help me find a job.

Aled: Oh she'll do it then. Nothing gets in her way.

Me: She says I'm family now.

Aled: Well you are.

Me: I've never met her before!

Aled: You have now. Enjoy it. It's weird.

Chris rolled his eyes.

Aled: Also Gabriel says hi.

He was sent a picture of Gabriel covered in mud in their front garden, waving between planting new borders. Chris grinned, sent a hello back and closed the paper. All out of CVs, a copy of the local paper to peruse on the way home and make some calls about once he got back to Nailsea, and Suze on the case to find him a job.

He drained his cup and headed out.

The town was bustling with people now, and Chris made a mental note to avoid it on Saturday afternoons. The tide was high and the boats in the bay were clattering noisily, but it disappeared under the sounds of an old-fashioned train pulling into the little station with a shriek of brakes just as he arrived. Waiting for it to empty out and change drivers, Chris flicked through the jobs section one last time, just in case Suze wasn't as good as Aled gave her credit for.

And something caught his eye.

There was one final ad that he'd missed, tucked into the corner of the jobs section. The word 'volunteer' leapt out to push him away, yet another word reeled him back in.

"Constables?"

He'd never heard of special constables. Volunteer coppers. He didn't know such a thing existed. But the ad…

"Commit to only sixteen hours per month as a uniformed police officer with full powers," he murmured. "Develop new skills, gain valuable experience and discover what you're really made of."

It sounded like the army ads. They'd dragged Tim in, who'd in turn dragged Chris. And the army had never been what it was cracked up to be…but the ads hadn't been *wrong*, either. Despite how it had ended, and despite the fact that he'd never fitted in like the army promised, he'd still enjoyed it. He'd never regretted doing it.

And this was just a volunteer thing. He could walk away whenever he wanted if he didn't like it, right?

He took a picture with his phone and sent it to Gabriel with a simple, *Should I try it?* as the train revved up to begin its return journey. The reply arrived as he boarded—a supremely unhelpful *I do like a man in uniform!*—and Chris was left to stare at the picture of the ad and stew on it.

It wouldn't pay any bills. And he knew enough about policing to know that sixteen hours a month wasn't going to be neatly packaged into start and end times like a regular volunteer position. It would be time away from creating his vegetable garden, and cycling trips with Gabriel. And he'd probably be shitting himself in terror the whole time. No way he had the confidence to be a copper.

Did he?

Something about it called to him, and he typed the weblink into his phone browser as St Ives disappeared over the hilly horizon.

After all, he'd have to settle in and get to know the area. And there were worse ways to do it than behind the wheel of a police car.

Chapter Nineteen

Aled hung up and punched the air.

It didn't matter that he was on one of the very few coffee breaks he was going to get this week. It didn't matter that he was having to drive over to Manchester every day for this fucking conference. It didn't matter that he'd failed to argue his way out of it on the grounds of his impending resignation.

None of it mattered anymore because —

"Got an offer on the house," he told Imogen, and grinned.

"Oh! Congratulations! A good one?"

"Only a grand below asking price."

"Not bad at *all*."

"Give me a minute," he said when the doors opened and people began to flock back in to hear the next speaker. "Just going to text my partner and then I'll be with you. Save me a seat."

"Will do!"

Me: Accepted an offer on the house. Moving is a go!

He only had four weeks left at work, but Gabriel hadn't formally resigned yet. But now they had an offer, balls could start rolling — so to speak. It lifted his spirits plenty for the next dull diatribe, and he marched in and took his seat next to Imogen with actual, honest-to-God enthusiasm for the first time in years.

His brain whirred, though. He didn't listen to the case study comparison of multi-sector marketing in Singapore versus Sydney. He sure as hell wasn't taking notes on it, but doing the sums for getting a moving date together.

At the end of his four weeks, Aled was going to take a month off for the move, settling into Cornwall and finding his way around his new life. Gabriel was hoping to jump straight from one job to the next, but Aled wanted some time to himself. So if he kept the pressure up — and as the buyer had no chain of their own, he *could* — they could be shot of the house in Newmillardam in six weeks. With a bit of luck.

If they had a gap between the houses in Newmillardam and St Ives, they'd already decided to go south and set up in one of Tom's hotels for a few weeks in the interim. Chris had been surprisingly relaxed about the idea, and Gabriel had practically lived in hotels before anyway. That wasn't a problem.

Still, he'd rather not. He emailed the estate agent in St Ives and his solicitor with the details and some urging to get things going on their end. The surveys had been done already. The new mortgage in principle was agreed with the bank. The —

A text flashed up.

Gabriel: Yay! Good timing, too ;) I was in the mood for a celebration.

Aled fought to keep the smirk off his face.

Gabriel: Boss/secretary?

All right, he wasn't having that kind of conversation in the middle of a conference with Imogen and Steve two feet away. Aled was going to take the out. He got up and started to make his way past equally bored peers to the exit.

"Excuse me," he whispered. "Sorry, I've got to deal with this. Sorry. Sorry. Thank you. Sorry."

The lobby was empty. The receptionist threw him a sympathetic look.

"Lucky escape?"

"You have no idea," he chuckled, sinking into a chair and opening the message thread.

Me: Where did that come from?

Gabriel: In the mood ;) So yes?

Me: What kind of boss/secretary?

It wasn't one of their regular games. Gabriel usually wasn't remotely interested in Aled's suits, and Aled didn't really have a thing for office play.

Gabriel: Rough ;) FORCE ME. And then maybe some power play after for round two?

Me: An overnighter, then?

Gabriel: Sure if you like x

Me: Will this mood hold until Friday night? I'll be knackered out by the drive and no way I'm playing an overnighter with you and then coming back here for the final day.

Gabriel: No. Doesn't need to. See?

Aled's jaw sagged.

Not because the photo was plainly sent from a hotel room. Not because Gabriel was using the hotel's room service menu to hide a sensitive area, and the branding was the exact same branding as on all the conference papers. Not even because of the hint of a black lace bra glowing through Gabriel's lily-white top.

Because the top was a blouse.

A blouse atop a tiny skirt atop two long, lean legs clad in beige tights. High heels. Cleavage. Was that eyeshadow?

Me: Are you sure?

Aled could count on one hand the number of times Gabriel had done drag for him — zero. It was so off the table, Aled never asked. Gabriel had killer legs and could probably have Aled coming like a horny teenager if he paraded around the house in heels, but he didn't even own any. He didn't do women's clothing. *Ever.*

Me: You need to be absolutely sure Gabe

Gabriel: GABRIEL

Gabriel: And I'm sure

Gabriel: Promise. Green all the way.

Gabriel: So we good to go?

Me: I will not be able to look out for your dysphoria, you know that? Especially not looking like that!

He couldn't at the best of times. Aled was as cis as cis came. Years with Gabriel and he still didn't really understand it all. What would set him off and what wouldn't. He just obeyed the rules he'd been given — pronouns, no woman talk in sex, no asking for skirts — and trusted Gabriel to look after himself in that regard. And it had worked a charm. He'd never set off an attack that he knew of.

But danger was staring him in the face, even as lust was telling him to fucking go for it.

Gabriel: I know :) Trust me.

Trust him.

Gabriel: Room 415.

Gabriel: Colour?

Me: Green.

He headed for the lifts.

The room was on the fourth floor and the door was slightly ajar. Aled paused to adjust himself and drag a cool, almost cold persona around himself. His hottest fantasies were all based on violent force, but he had to distance himself a little first, lest they feel too real. A few deep breaths later, he knocked and opened the door.

Gabriel was sitting pretty at the desk, typing away on Aled's laptop from home. Aled locked the door and leaned up against it, staring. Good God, he'd figured Gabriel probably looked nice in a skirt with those cyclist's legs, but he'd been wrong. Gabriel looked fan-fucking-tastic.

Fucking being the operative word.

"Something wrong, Mr Evans?"

"No," he said. "Just a long presentation." He began to work off his tie. "How's that report coming along?"

"Almost done."

"Time for a break, I think. Put the kettle on, won't you?"

"Of course!"

As Gabriel sashayed over to the kettle — shockingly natural in the heels — Aled sidled over to the laptop and closed the lid, dragging the chair back and sitting in it himself. When Gabriel came back with two cups of tea and blinked at the chair, Aled simply gestured at the desk.

"Pull up a pew. Let's chat."

"Okay."

He eyed those long legs once more as Gabriel perched on the edge of the desk.

"How long have you been working with me now?"

"Five years," Gabriel said.

"Mm. Surprised you've never applied for a more senior position."

"I like my job," Gabriel said, sipping at his tea. "It suits me perfectly."

"And yet this is the first time you've agreed to come to a conference with me."

"Well, my partner's never been totally comfortable with it," Gabriel admitted. "You know, going away with your boss and everything. But we're not an item anymore, so…"

Aled hummed, rising casually and putting his untouched tea back on top of the minibar. When he returned, he stopped right in front of Gabriel and lightly touched his knee.

"And why is that?"

"Is—is that important, sir?"

"No." He took the saucer. Gabriel let go in surprise, and Aled put the tea aside. "I suppose it isn't."

Then he slid an arm around Gabriel's waist and kissed him.

Instantly, Gabriel went rigid. Arms shoved at Aled's chest. Legs tried to close and push his torso out, but too late. A muffled squeak interrupted the kiss and Gabriel wrenched his head away.

"Sir!"

"Oh, don't pretend this wasn't what you were after all along," Aled said dismissively.

He fisted his other hand in Gabriel's hair and kissed him again, yanking his head back and his chest in until Gabriel was left with no option but to open his mouth. He squirmed and whimpered but didn't try to scream.

Aled soon abandoned the mouth for the neck, sinking his teeth in deep and grinding his stiffening cock against Gabriel's hips with every breathless plea for him to stop. He could feel breasts. The firm lace of the bra. Soft thighs. Hands still pushing, but the resistance weakening as Gabriel tired.

"God, you smell good. Wore your best perfume as well as your best shoes? You know how to get a man's interest."

"Mr Evans, please stop—"

"Stop?" Aled chuckled. "We've both wanted this for years. Why on earth would I stop?"

He kissed him again, cutting off the answer, then dragged him by the hair to the bed. Face-down was easiest. And once there, getting those slender wrists bound with Aled's tie was child's play.

"There," Aled said, once Gabriel was wrenching uselessly against the probably-ruined silk tie. He turned him over and kissed him once more, settling his weight over Gabriel's legs and kissing his neck like a lover. "Relax."

"Please, please, you don't have to do this, *please* — "

"Of course I don't have to," Aled said. "But we both want to."

"I don't! I don't, *please* — "

"Cute, but you do," Aled said, kissing his way down that straining neck and beginning to finger the buttons on the blouse. "Casually mentioning that you're single while sitting on my desk in those clothes?"

"That's not — "

"Of course it's what you meant," Aled taunted, ripping open the blouse and laughing at the bra. "Look at this. Front opening. You really *do* want it bad."

"I don't!"

"Nobody wears one of these unless they want fucked," Aled scoffed. He twisted Gabriel's head in for another kiss, licking around his mouth when he clamped his jaw shut. "Fuck, I like them fierce. You can suck me off another time, it's fine. I get it. Not everyone likes that sort of thing. Those tits more than make up for it, though." He pinched the nipple ring, and Gabriel gasped. Aled took the opportunity to plunder his mouth before pulling off with a chuckle. "See?

Gorgeous tits. Don't worry, sweetheart, I'll make the most of them."

He unclipped the bra and opened it, massaging the freed breasts briefly before kissing his way down Gabriel's squirming body. He dragged the tights, knickers and skirt off, Gabriel kicking wildly the whole time, then sat on his shins to force the heels back onto his feet.

"I like heels," he said, then held them down and open to turn and get himself inescapably between Gabriel's thighs. "Especially on gorgeous pieces of meat like you. You can keep those on while I fuck you."

"Oh God, oh God, oh God —"

Aled held Gabriel down with his own body, biting and bruising a breast as he worked his cock out of his trousers and boxers. Thank God for buttonhole flies. He shifted up to wring kisses out of Gabriel's begging mouth as he rubbed his dick against his belly to get it fully hard, then pulled back and slapped the thighs spread around his own hips.

"All right, gorgeous. Here goes."

He sank into hot, wet heat like soaking in a Jacuzzi after a long day. The squirming was the jets. The whimpering under his palm was ecstasy. The muted sob as he bottomed out was perfect.

"Fuck," he whispered. "You were fucking made for my dick, you know that?"

Gabriel just cried. The fight had drained away, and Aled let a couple of idle thrusts out to loosen him up before pushing up on his hands and knees.

"Come on," he said. "Legs around my waist."

"No."

The slap was almost casual.

"Do it. I want to see those tits dance."

"Fuck you, fuck you, fuck you—"

"That's what you're doing, gorgeous."

Gabriel didn't much get off on being slapped, so another two or three was all it took before those heels were locked around Aled's back. He fucked hard and fast, doing exactly as he'd promised. Gabriel didn't often let his boobs jiggle like that, and Aled fully intended on seizing the opportunity.

And biting them a few times, too.

But he wasn't going to all this effort for a quick rut. Why not tie him open and fist-fuck him until he agreed to anything? Like sucking dick. He'd bite otherwise, even if it was a game.

Aled pulled out as an idea occurred. There'd be a dressing gown or a bathrobe in here somewhere. Why not put the cord to use? Undo his hands, tie his legs open to the bedpost, and fuck him with whatever was in reach until he offered to suck dick for his way out?

"Wait here," he said.

Of course, Gabriel didn't. The moment Aled turned his back on the bed, the mattress bounced. He swung around as Gabriel pelted for the door—but the tie foiled him. He sobbed as he backed into it, fingers scrabbling uselessly at the knob, then bolted into the bathroom as Aled made for him. He couldn't close it fast enough. Aled shouldered his way inside, then slammed and locked the door behind himself.

He smiled at the two bathrobes, hanging from the hooks.

Then wiped it off his face and turned to Gabriel.

"I'm running out of patience."

"Please let me go. Please! I won't tell anyone, I won't do anything, I'll just quit and—"

"Quit? Best secretary I've ever had? I don't think so. You'll be sitting at your desk on Monday morning, and sitting on my dick at lunchtime. No more pretending. Got it?"

"Ple—"

"And there's a new dress code," he said, turning on the shower before sliding one of the bathrobe cords free. "You can keep the bra—it's a sexy touch. But the knickers go. And the tights. No point. And you start bringing your makeup kit to work. Sucking dick smears your lipstick."

Gabriel burst into tears as Aled gagged him with the cord, and didn't fight as he was bundled into the shower, still in his high heels, and pressed face first into the cold tiles.

"Open your legs."

They closed.

Aled leaned in.

"If you'd stayed on the bed," he whispered, "then I would have come in your cunt like you asked me to, and that would have been the end of it. But you wanted to play silly little games instead. Now I don't want to hurt you, but if you don't open your legs, I'm going to assume that you're asking me to."

They remained tightly closed.

"Never would have taken you for a pain slut," Aled quipped, leaning his chest against Gabriel's back to keep him in place. "Always thought you were proud of your cock-riding abilities. Guess you never can tell, huh?"

A muffled whimper escaped the gag as Aled prised those tight arse cheeks apart, and Gabriel opened his legs as Aled—roughly—pushed a finger into his arse.

The no was audible. The absence of a safeword was even louder.

"Too late now, sweetheart. You asked for pain. This is gonna do the trick."

He worked him open with soap and fingers, then turned him around. Tucking his elbows under Gabriel's knees, Aled lifted until Gabriel hung between him and the bathroom wall, heels dangling limply in the air, and utterly helpless.

"Next time you run, it'll go in dry," he said—and dropped him right onto Aled's dick.

It was a hard, brutal fuck. Tighter than the bed. Tighter than the fingering. He leaned back and watched impassively as he bucked his hips again and again and again. No more teasing. No more taunting. This time he was going to come.

And Gabriel was going to learn a lesson.

It didn't take long—the pressure, the squirming, the muffled sobs. He stayed buried inside until Gabriel's twitching body had milked him of every last drop, then pulled out and slid Gabriel down into the bath. He ripped off the cord and tilted his chin up with two fingers.

"Does that hurt?"

Gabriel nodded, gulping back tears.

"What did I say?"

"N-next time, it g-goes in dry."

"You want that?"

"N-no."

"So tell me what you do want."

Gabriel opened his mouth. Aled raised an eyebrow. Slowly, those dark eyes dropped.

"To—"

"Look at me, you little whore."

His gaze snapped up again.

"Now, what were you about to say?"

"I — I want to — to — "

"Yes?"

"I want to suck your dick. And then go home. Please."

"You want to suck my dick?"

"Y-yes. And — "

"Good. Now get out and kneel on the bathmat."

Gabriel crawled out, and Aled dried off and donned a bathrobe before unlocking the door.

"Crawl to the bed, then take your shoes off."

He had to shuffle on his knees, thanks to the sodden tie, but the heels were reasonably loose and came off easily. Aled sat down on the edge of the bed, towelling his hair, and eyed Gabriel imperiously.

"Pretty little thing, but you're dumb as soup," he remarked cruelly, then tossed the towel aside and sat back against the pillows, kicking his feet up onto the sheets. "Get up here."

Gabriel climbed up onto the bed and knelt at the end, as far as humanly possible without falling off. Aled rolled his eyes.

"Get over here and open my belt with your teeth."

It was difficult, and meant to be. Gabriel nearly fell off the bed more than once before he managed it, and Aled did nothing to help. They had eased from the rough play to the coercive play, his preferred territory, and he had every intention of making it last. He liked a mindfuck just as much as the real fuck, and there was none of that in just holding Gabriel down and *making* him take it.

No, getting Gabriel to fuck himself was the best part.

"Kiss me."

The first attempt was a sharp peck, and Aled knocked him sideways with the slap.

"Like a lover. Like you wanted."

"I—"

"One more argument out of you, and I'll fuck your back door until it breaks."

Gabriel dropped his gaze, leaned in and kissed him. It was almost romantic.

"Good," Aled murmured when he pulled away. "Now kiss your way down until you get to my dick, and make love to it with your mouth like the cocksucking bitch you are."

Gabriel's abdomen flexed with the aborted attempt at an orgasm, and Aled smirked to himself. There was no need to fuck him again. He was about to go off at any moment.

Progress was slow, but there was only so long Gabriel could drag it out. And Aled was already half-hard again, so only a few tentative sucks brought him fully back to life.

"Good," he murmured, stroking his fingers through wet hair. "Let's see how much practice you've been getting."

It was the only warning Gabriel got before Aled pushed down on the back of his neck and forced him to deepthroat. Aled didn't really care about it for the sake of a blowjob—it was the shiver in Gabriel's spine that did it, the frozen fear, the way he could almost *hear* the panic of being unable to breathe...

He fisted his hand in Gabriel's hair and pulled him up just enough to breathe.

"Been on your knees for a few men?"

Gabriel hummed. Aled clenched his jaw as the vibration threatened to end things early, and waited until it stopped.

"Might come in handy next time I have a meeting with the board. Ever sucked fifteen old men off in a row?"

A whimper.

"You'll figure it out. Let's try again, shall we?"

And he pushed once more.

He repeated it two or three times, each longer than the last, before deciding that he was recovered enough from the shower fuck for something a little more fun.

"All right, that's enough. Better places for that. Now, you ready to learn a few lines for me?"

He let Gabriel pull off his dick, but kept a hand fisted in his damp hair.

"Answer me."

"I—I don't understand."

"You're going to ride me like a bitch in heat, and you're going to say some pretty words while you do it. Or"—he leaned forward and tweaked the bound hands—"we're right back to square one, aren't we, sweetheart?"

Gabriel took a shuddering breath, then nodded.

"Come on, then. Climb aboard."

Gabriel pushed up onto his knees, and Aled guided him into position until he hovered perfectly above Aled's cock.

Then Aled spread his arms along the headboard, and smirked.

"Tell me you want my cock."

"I—I want your cock. Sir."

"Again. Tell me what you want."

"I want your cock."

"Sit down, then."

The slow slide of tight heat was excruciatingly good, and Aled could have echoed the little whine that escaped as Gabriel got to the root. But he didn't. Instead, he reached out and tugged on a hard nipple.

"Look at you, all turned on."

Wisely, Gabriel said nothing.

"Tell me it's too big."

"It—it's too big."

"No, no, no. Look, I know a whore like you has had a thousand cocks before, but you surely know how to stroke a man's ego? Come on. Again."

Gabriel took a deep breath, then delivered the line in a husky voice that *did* things.

"Much better. Now start fucking it."

Of course, the first attempt was little more than a roll of the hips, and Aled tutted. That was all he needed to do. The second time, his cock almost slipped out before Gabriel slammed his hips back down, and the headboard clapped the wall.

"Very good, sweetheart. Keep it up. Yes, that's right. You're getting it."

In fact, the in-and-out did little for Aled in this position. He preferred the hip rolling if Gabriel were sitting in his lap. But he had no intention of coming here.

"Tell me to fuck you a new hole."

"Oh *God*. Fuck me a new hole."

"Nice touch. Now would a slut like you want to be doing all the work? Seems a little fake. Tell me to fondle your tits."

"Mm. Fuck, that's so good. Touch me. Grab my tits. *Fuck* yes—"

Aled grinned, not moving a muscle to do it.

"Nice performance, darling. Mix it up a little. What was the first line again?"

"Oh fuck, it's so big. It's so big! Mm, fuck. Harder. Fuck me a new hole!"

Grinning, Aled reached forward and grabbed a handful of hair, dragging Gabriel into a sharp kiss — before throwing him sideways.

"You'd make a good porn star," he said. "Maybe I don't need a secretary. Plenty of tarts in short skirts around. Why should I pay you when a studio would pay me to borrow you for a day's filming, huh?"

"No," Gabriel whispered.

"No, what?"

"J-just you, sir. Just you."

"Cute. Okay, I think it's time for the show. Bathroom."

"What?"

"Bathroom. Go."

Gabriel didn't try for the door this time. He trailed into the en suite like a well-trained pet, even waiting in there while Aled gathered a few things from the safe. The hope that sparked in his eyes when Aled threw his bra, blouse and skirt down on the counter died the moment he realised there were no knickers.

"Going to make ourselves a little movie."

Gabriel closed his eyes.

"You're going to put your bra and skirt on, then bend over the counter and look me in the eye. You don't close your eyes. You don't look away. And you don't forget your lines. Make a good movie, and we're done here. But" — Aled wiggled his phone — "we will keep doing this until we make a good movie. Understood?"

"Y-yes."

"Yes what?"

"Yes, Mr Evans."

"Good."

Aled locked the bathroom door and put his shirt and tie back on, smoothing them into perfect place as Gabriel dressed and tidied his rumpled hair. Aled turned him for a deep kiss that went unresisted, then unbuttoned the blouse again and bent him over the counter.

"Remember your lines?"

"Yes, Mr Evans."

"Good. Let's get started then, shall we? Why don't you tell me what you want, sweetheart?"

He held up the phone to the mirror and rubbed his cock against the back of Gabriel's skirt.

"Come on," he coaxed. "What do you want?"

Gabriel bit his lip and took a shuddering breath before reciting the words.

"I want your cock," he whispered. "Please, God, I want you to fuck me like — *ohmyfuckingGod!*"

The yell was beautiful. The grip of Gabriel's arse around the head of Aled's cock was heaven. He squeezed bruises into narrow hips and barely held off from coming on the spot.

"Oh fuck, it's so big! It's too big!"

"Just relax, darling. You still want it?"

"Y-yes. Yes. Fuck me a new ho — *oh!*"

He didn't stop, that time. Drove all the way into that tight body like he'd die if he didn't. Gabriel's head bowed momentarily before he snapped it back up, and Aled decided to forgive the rule-breaking on the basis of the ecstatic moan he made instead.

"Oh God, harder. Harder! Fuck me harder!"

He did. The yowl was definitely one of pain, but then Gabriel shoved a hand below the counter and began to jack himself.

"Fuck, I'm so close. I'm so close. Squeeze my tit. *Fuck*."

Aled ripped the cup down, yanking on the nipple ring before seizing the entire breast and holding it still while the other bounced with the force of his thrusts.

Then Gabriel surprised him.

Gabriel, who didn't like anal and usually got off later, got off.

It hit him like a freight train, and the spasm nearly knocked them both from the counter. The pressure was incredible, and Aled's climax was both inevitable and hard-won. He ground up into Gabriel's hips as the world wavered around the edges—then released the phone and saved the footage.

"Fuck," he panted. "*Fuck*."

Gabriel slipped from his dick in a messy rush and sat down hard on the floor.

"Game over," Aled panted.

"What? No! Can't we—"

"Sorry," Aled whispered, sliding down to sit on the tiles beside him. Gabriel instantly climbed into his naked lap, kissing his jaw hopefully. "Sorry, sweetheart. Another time. It's a red for me."

"You okay?" Gabriel whispered.

"Yeah. *Fuck* yeah. Just done."

Gabriel dashed their noses together, and Aled opened one eye to smile at him.

"Best game ever," Gabriel whispered.

"Yeah?"

"Hello, wanting to carry on here?"

Aled laughed.

"You sure you're okay?" Gabriel whispered, carding his fingers through Aled's hair. "Need a cuddle or anything?"

"Yes please, but I am sure, too," Aled murmured, sighing when Gabriel twisted sideways and kissed his ear, the hopeful lap-straddling turning into a cuddle against the side of the bath, like they were dozing on the sofa at home. "I just think another round might kill my dick. And I had a bit of a twinge when you just walked in here without a fight, so best stop now before the doubts show up."

"Okay," Gabriel said. "Think I'll go full cuddle mode anyway. That was the hottest game we've ever played—I am so keeping that suit and I may go and make up an entire backstory for us when we play it."

Aled tipped his head back against the bath with a smile, stroking Gabriel's bare thigh. He needed a piss. Gabriel was leaking cum and probably a fair amount of blood. They were going to check out *fast* before the hotel could discover the ruined bed.

"If I got that at every conference, they'd never keep me in the office," he murmured.

"Need a secretary at Tom's hotel chain?"

Aled laughed. "Oh please, like you're not already going to take advantage of your mate's hotels."

"Pot, kettle."

"True."

"Get a list of them. We'll cross them off. Like bingo."

Aled squeezed, kissed the top of Gabriel's head, then patted his thigh and let go. "Come on. Nature calls. Then a sex-free shower."

"Can I join you anyway?"

"Bringing some kisses?"

"Yep."

"Join away."

He did insist on getting the first aid kit on Gabriel's abused bits first, but then was followed into the shower by warm kisses and unbridled affection. Aled wasn't sure if it was aftercare or just Gabriel riding a high, but he didn't really care. It was nice. It smothered the flicker of doubt like a shield on a candle flame, and neatly partitioned the sex game off from the rest of his life. It had been fun. No safewords used. And Gabriel was cuddling up like they were on a honeymoon.

"Thanks," he whispered into ink-black hair.

"Welcome."

"Let's see if we can't have a little fun after my last day at work."

"Ooh, *yes.*"

Chapter Twenty

Once they had the offer, things went *fast*.

Gabriel didn't know the first thing about moving house or chains or mortgage agreements, and he didn't have to. All he knew was that Aled came home from work one day, said they had a moving date, and that was the end of it.

So Gabriel handed in his notice at work, texted Suze about whether she'd had any luck finding him something new, and got ready to go.

The nerves were building, but there was a thick layer of excitement, too. Once, he would have been too terrified to move an inch without a new job in place. Once, the idea of being unemployed and relying on just Aled's income had been scary beyond belief.

Now, he just crossed his fingers it wouldn't last too long and carried on researching cycling routes and spying on Cornish Grindr on his lunch breaks.

And so the weeks rolled by, until –

Until the end.

Gabriel's last day of work was a Wednesday.

They'd booked the moving van for Friday, and Gabriel had opted to stay and help Aled move rather than go down to Nailsea and help Chris. Chris had far less stuff, and Aled had a dodgy back. It only made sense.

And so his last day at the gym was a Wednesday.

It was an early shift too, from seven until three. Gabriel usually wasn't too keen on the early shift, but at least it meant his leaving party was cake and a bit of a fuss at lunchtime instead of stopping them from dragging him to a pub. His colleagues were nice and all, but they *really* didn't understand alcoholism.

But he wasn't expecting Aled to walk in just after two.

Whenever Aled came to the gym, they mutually ignored one another. Gabriel liked this job too much to risk it by screwing on the premises. Oh, he'd fucked in Aled's car in the car park after work occasionally, but that was off-shift and in a vehicle with blacked-out windows. He'd never done it in the building, and he and Aled — at most — gave a bland nod of recognition when they saw each other inside.

As far as Gabriel's colleagues knew, he had nothing to do with the ginger guy who used the pool three times a week.

They exchanged nods as always, but Gabriel's slight suspicion that Aled was up to something escalated when he walked up the stairs. The pool was downstairs. Nothing Aled ever bothered using was upstairs. And sure enough, seconds later, Gabriel's phone vibrated in his pocket.

Aled: Upstairs toilet.

Gabriel's pulse quickened. Called it. Aled was going to break the rules on his last day in the building. What a bastard.

But then…why not? He glanced around. The gym was quiet. The rush wouldn't start until after four. And the toilets—for obvious reasons—didn't have any cameras in them. If they were *quick…*

He slid his phone back into his pocket, checked his radio and hefted his bucket up.

"Going to get the loos wiped down before the rush," he said to Emily. "Give me a buzz if you need anything up front."

"Sure thing, sweetie."

He meandered up the stairs like nothing was amiss. The upstairs toilets were tucked away towards the back of the building, two small bathrooms opposite the yoga studio that were little more than small tiled squares with a toilet, a sink, a permanently broken hand-dryer and some disability aids so the gym could claim to be accessible. Despite them being upstairs and the only lift in the building breaking down every other day.

Aled was waiting outside the yoga studio with a sports bag at his feet, and texting on his phone. He ignored Gabriel, so Gabriel ignored him in return. Dropping the *closed for cleaning* sign outside the men's room door, he rapped his knuckles on the wood, just in case anyone was preening, and walked in with the bucket and mop to start cleaning. His phone buzzed as he closed the door behind him, and his throat went dry.

It wasn't his first time in a public toilet, but it would be his first time in *this* public toilet.

Aled: Continuation of the conference game.

Oh, *fuck* yes!

Aled: Boss finds secretary's second job.

Aled: Colour?

He had to ask?

Me: Green green green green green!

That had been the best game they'd ever played, bar none, and Gabriel was wet just at the thought of it. His hands shook as he squeezed out the mop and started cleaning the floor. What was Aled going to do? Fuck his face and come on his T-shirt so Gabriel had to get the spunk off before leaving the toilets and make up some story about splashing himself with the tap? Or make another sex video? Or *threaten* to? After all, Gabriel was in his work uniform this time. And —

The door opened and closed, and the lock clicked.

"Well, well, well."

Gabriel straightened up and stiffened at the predatory smile on Aled's face.

"I thought it was you," Aled murmured, looking him up and down in a manner that made Gabriel's cheeks flush. "Second job?"

"What are you doing here?"

"Getting laid," Aled drawled. "Is this why you only do part-time at the office?"

"Yes, s-sir. Y-you shouldn't—"

"Not anymore," Aled said. "You'll be starting full time at the office on Monday as my personal assistant."

"B-but—"

Aled cocked his head, smirking. "Oh, I get it. You *do* want that nice video we made doing the rounds. Well —" He turned away, unlocking the door. "I can go down to the front desk right now and show them if you —"

"*No.*"

Aled paused.

"Lock it," Gabriel whispered.

The lock clunked loudly.

"What do you want?"

"I want you to do your damn job," Aled drawled. "And that's not cleaning toilets. It's meeting my every need."

Gabriel took a long, shuddering breath.

"W-what do you need, sir?"

"That's not very polite. Try again."

"W-what —" He licked his lips. "How may I be of service, sir?"

"Better," Aled purred. "You can start by losing the trousers. There should *never* be clothes in my way when I want to fuck you."

Gabriel knew these games. They were all about anticipation. Aled wasn't going to touch him. He wasn't going to hit him or hurt him. Instead, he was going to sit back and blackmail his victim into doing all the hard work themselves — and then say they liked it, because if they hadn't, they wouldn't have done it.

It was a complete mindfuck, and Gabriel *loved* it.

He worked off his trainers, then stepped out of his trousers — and then his underwear when Aled raised his eyebrows. The bathroom was cold, and Gabriel shivered in just his polo shirt and socks. He ached for a kiss, but knew full well he wasn't going to get one. Sex toys like him didn't get kisses.

And Aled said, "I'm not going to fuck you."

"W-what?"

Was Gabriel going to have to fuck himself on Aled's dick? Wank for him on camera? Suck him off on his knees on the hard, cold tiles?

"Hands on the sink and bend over."

Gabriel bit his lip, but turned his back and did as he was told. Aled casually kicked his legs farther apart and Gabriel hiccupped a shaky breath. A toy. He was going to get fucked with a toy instead. Or even Aled's hand, if he felt *really* sadistic. Would he really fist Gabriel at work? Would he —

Gabriel barely stopped the shout from escaping when cold silicon touched his labia. Cold, dry, *wide* silicon. He knew what it was just from the touch.

His favourite ribbed dildo. The one that he used to masturbate if nobody was home and he itched too much for a simple hand job to do the trick. The one that touched him in *all* the right places.

The one that was just a shade too wide to be comfortable without lube.

And, of course, Aled hadn't bothered with *that*.

"Fuck-fuck-fuck-fuck..." Gabriel whispered, fingers tightening on the rim of the sink until they turned white with the pressure.

"Later."

It ached, but his dick swelled. It burned, but his blood did too. When it bottomed out and Aled's chuckle was icy-cold and cruel in the freezing room, Gabriel realised he'd been wriggling to get it deeper, and blushed to the roots of his hair.

"Don't look so embarrassed," Aled murmured, leaning in to kiss his ear as he twisted the dildo inside until Gabriel's knees shook. "This is nothing compared to that little video."

"Please stop…"

"No chance."

Aled abandoned him for a moment, and the sports bag he'd dumped by the door rustled. Gabriel dropped his head, gulping for air against the lust that was coursing through him. *Jesus*, he wanted to fuck. He wanted to tackle Aled to the floor and demand a blowjob at the very least.

But then he heard metal clink, and his heart sank.

Sure enough, the chilly confines of the chastity belt were locked into place, and Gabriel blinked back frustrated tears as Aled tightened the straps and secured it. The key was pressed to Gabriel's lips for him to kiss, then vanished into Aled's pocket.

"Put your clothes back on. Disgusting little whore."

The insult scraped along the edges of Gabriel's kink, and he shivered.

"You finish your shift. You speak to nobody about this. And when you're done, I'll be waiting outside. You get in my car, and then what happens is up to you."

"Up—up to me?"

He didn't believe it. Of course he didn't believe it. And when Aled smirked, Gabriel knew that he was right to be suspicious.

"You can kiss me like a lover and be treated like a high-class whore. Or you can put up a fight and I can break those pretty wrists in a pair of police-issue handcuffs and fuck you like the gutter trash you are. Up to you. But either way—"

His hand lashed out. Gabriel's jaw was seized in a painful grip, and the kiss he'd wanted was savage and sore.

"You don't work here anymore," Aled hissed. "Understood?"

Gabriel stared into cold eyes and swallowed back the hot rush of want.

"Yes, sir."

Chapter Twenty-One

Chris arrived at the crack of dawn.

Teen years stacking shelves and moving pallets in a warehouse hadn't been entirely forgotten—with the aid of a furniture dolly pinched from the garage, he'd loaded up a hire van in the early hours and dropped his keys through the solicitors' office door before four in the morning.

Why not make use of the insomnia?

He'd been born and raised in Somerset, yet the sight of its dark, low hills fading in the rear-view mirror did nothing. The sight of Cornwall rising before him under the grey pre-dawn light creeping across the sky, though—that brought a lump to his throat. When he left the arterial route and began to follow the sat nav through winding country lanes and high hedgerows, it felt a little like abandoning the route his entire life had been on and forging ahead with a new one.

And it was fucking *scary*.

He had never expected a chance meeting at a race to lead to this. He'd almost talked himself out of saying hello to the pretty cyclist with the dark eyes. Something had had him tongue-tied, even while his brain insisted that his sexuality made asking Gabriel out a terrible idea. That insistence had rung for years, and yet something about Gabriel had let him ignore it long enough to find out it had never been true.

But it wasn't supposed to have happened.

And it wasn't supposed to have led him here.

Not Cornish country roads and a new home in the fields with a good friend and loving boyfriend just across the yard. Not—

Not happiness, and Christ if that wasn't a complex mix of pride and embarrassment at admitting that to himself.

As he guided the hire van through the warren of roads to his new house, Noodle crying plaintively in the carrier on the passenger seat, Chris wondered if anyone could possibly have predicted this. He'd been an awkward kid, a shit soldier, a lonely adult and he'd never deliberately made a friend in his life. But Gabriel had swept him away, and now here he was. Pulling up in thick fog to a closed gate ten yards back from a narrowing country lane that would become as familiar as the back of his own hand.

He cut the engine and got out to open the gate.

The sun was a pale disc on the very lip of the horizon, weak and feeble through the fog. The silence was both calming and unnerving. Hedges loomed darkly around the plot. The keys felt strange in his hand, and the bungalow was deafeningly silent when he unlocked the door.

"Home sweet home," he muttered.

His voice echoed in the empty space, and he paced through each of the empty rooms, mentally mapping where his life would go. The master bedroom could be a gaming den. His bed could go under the window that peeked out at the yard. He could turn the bland beige and white into something better, something more personal, something more *permanent*.

He paced back to the van and drove it through the silence until the back lined up perfectly with the front door.

Then he sat back, cut the ignition and let the quiet claim him for just a moment longer.

"Home sweet home," he whispered once more — and it didn't feel quite so strange.

Rather than starting with the heavy furniture or settling the annoyed cat, Chris unlocked the back doors of the van and found a small shoebox of photographs. Start small. Start feeling like this was *real*.

He lined them up on the bedroom windowsill — Mum, Tim, his passing out parade, Gabriel, Snowdonia at sunrise — then headed back to the van to retrieve his dismantled bed. Noodle cried from the carrier in the passenger seat, but Chris opted to let the cat be until he was done to-ing and fro-ing from the van. He could get himself set up, then sit back with Noodle in their new house and wait for the rest of the pieces to fall into place.

Aled and Gabriel were setting off today, but likely wouldn't arrive until the evening. Their moving van might not even make it until the next day. The provisional plan was that they'd show up with enough in the car for that first night, and if the removal van didn't make it, then they'd set up a tent in the yard and they could spent their first night in Cornwall camping in their new garden, with a campfire under the stars and—Chris suspected—the first of many experiments as to which fast food joints in St Ives were any good.

Chris preferred that plan to all moving in at once. He had a little space to adjust and get his thoughts in order before they showed up and the enormity of it all really sank in. By the time they arrived, he'd have started to get used to everything.

He was starting his life over anew.

Being busy helped keep the nagging anxiety at bay. He put the bed together but nothing else, instead stacking everything room by room and watching the van's load shrinking with every trip. He got the vehicle almost completely unloaded before he got to the plastic bag hidden at the very back, and it made him pause.

A lump formed in his throat as he picked it up.

He ought to start putting all the furniture back together and in the right places, but—

The one attachment he'd held to the bungalow was that his brother's ashes had been scattered in the garden after he was killed. Chris had scattered Mum there too. It had felt right. She'd mourned Tim for the rest of her life, and Chris didn't believe in an afterlife, but it had felt right to put them together in the garden once more.

But just leaving them there hadn't.

So before he'd left, he'd dug up a bucket of earth from the vegetable patch and had two brass plaques made. He obviously couldn't find every speck of ash again, but he could take part of the garden itself with him. He could let them rest in peace, but not leave them behind. He could replant their memory.

He'd meant to wait to put his plan into action, but—

But standing in the silent plot under the slowly strengthening sun, clutching the bag and its contents to his chest, Chris was struck with the urge to do it *now*.

He put the bag back and shut the rear doors before rescuing Noodle. The cat hid in the back of the carrier, wailing but refusing to come out when he set it down and opened the door in the kitchen. Shrugging, he laid out food, water and a litter tray, closed the kitchen door so there'd be no escaping and trying to flee back to Somerset, then locked up the bungalow and headed out. Left out of the driveway led to a single-track road and more Cornwall. Right headed back to St Ives.

He turned right, and went looking for a garden centre.

Chris wanted to take up gardening. Have a vegetable plot. A fruit tree or two. Grow some of his own necessities. Maybe even keep chickens, now they'd bought a big enough plot. He'd always liked the idea of being a bit self-sufficient, so he'd already looked up garden centres around the St Ives area. Trundling through the quiet town at half past nine, a sense of belonging was already starting to settle over him. He could see tomato plants overhanging garden walls and peas dying back along trellises. He could find company here. Maybe even work along those lines. He'd never thought about going into landscaping, but there was bound to be somebody who could take him on. He filed the thought away, and the strange land started to seem a little more familiar.

It was about half-eight, and the town was awake, if not exactly buzzing. He paused to grab a coffee from a local cafe and pick up a fistful of leaflets on community clubs and events, then continued to a small garden centre just on the other side of the bay. It didn't have much, but it had what he needed—a rear yard filled with saplings, and massive bags of the appropriate composts. He bought two trees and enough dirt to bury a corpse. Cherry trees, of course. Mum had always liked the flowers, and Tim had liked the fruit.

He spent the rest of the morning planting them on either side of the gate with the earth from the bungalow garden.

In the peaceful quiet, the jarring sensation of starting again eased. Birds cheeped in the hedge, curious about what he was doing. He could put up feeders. Noodle was too old to be bothered about going out much anymore. His vegetable garden could run down the grassy area between his bungalow and the gate, and Aled and Gabriel could do something with their own narrow run. Then the open yard between the two front doors could be a communal whatever. Patio furniture, he imagined. The hammock. Something to enjoy the long summer evenings together, surrounded by bees and goldfinches and fat chickens scratching in the dirt. He could grow strawberries and runner beans and try and sneak things into Aled's food so he wouldn't just drop dead of a heart attack in twenty years' time.

Sitting back on his heels, saplings planted, Chris bit his lip at the thought of being here in twenty years.

Reaching for the abandoned bag, he slid out the brass plaques and set one at the base of each tree with tears blurring his vision. It didn't matter. He knew what they said.

Timothy James Wheeler.
Karen Mary Wheeler.

They shimmered in the sun, the letters dancing before his eyes. An odd warmth sat at each shoulder, as though they were with him. Chris didn't even believe in ghosts, yet something compelled him to speak.

"Think I did good?" he whispered.

No, history told him. Mum wouldn't have liked this triad situation. Tim would have been weird about it.

But—

Their loss. Maybe in time they'd have come around. Maybe they wouldn't. But *Chris* knew he'd done good. He had a nice house in the country, a friend across the garden and a boyfriend flitting between the pair of them without a care in the world. He had a plan for the future and a job lined up for the short term. His bike was ready in the hall for the first trip out with Gabriel, and his cat was hiding in a carrier in the kitchen, waiting for nightfall to explore.

Gabriel: Setting off now. Let me know when you get there. See you this evening!!! Xxx

Chris smiled and tapped out a reply.

Me: Already here and moving myself in x

He'd done good.

Chapter Twenty-Two

Gabriel: Did you pack your suit?

It wasn't a question Aled expected after being kicked out of the house to buy — of all things — washing up liquid. Gabriel had gotten tired of his triple-checking everything and thrown him out so Gabriel could finish boxing up their last odds and ends. He wasn't to come back until he'd found a very particular type of washing up liquid that, four supermarkets later, Aled was beginning to suspect didn't exist.

Me: Sort of. It's in its bag, hanging up underneath the coats.

Gabriel: Okay :) You can come back to the house now. But you pull up outside like a taxi, text me that you're here, and we're going out.

Me: We are?

Gabriel: Yes.

Aled rolled his eyes and put the washing up liquid back on the shelf. No doubt Gabriel had a plan in mind. Maybe this was what the social side of being a sub felt like.

Still, he wasn't about to argue. Tomorrow's chaos had his stomach in a knot. The 'what if's wouldn't stop bothering him. They'd played a game almost every day for the past two weeks, either to calm Aled's nerves or lance some of Gabriel's excitement. If Gabriel was about to propose something filthy in a public setting to take his mind off it, Aled wasn't going to put up much of a fight.

He got home just after two, and dutifully sent the text. To his surprise, Gabriel emerged with a case in tow and one of Aled's suits thrown over his shoulder in its bag. Not the work suit either, but the *really* nice suit. The one he'd worn to Suze's wedding and Nan's funeral.

"What are you up to?" Aled asked once Gabriel had put them in the boot and let himself into the passenger side.

"Taking your mind off tomorrow," Gabriel replied breezily. "We have a fancy evening booked."

"We do?"

"Yep." Gabriel was already programming the sat nav. "Okay. Go!"

"Are you going to tell me what we're doing?"

"When we get there."

Aled rolled his eyes, but turned the car around and followed the instructions. Gabriel had only put in a postcode near Birstall, and Aled wasn't in the habit of cruising around Birstall unless it was to go to IKEA.

And somehow he didn't think Gabriel had brought the suit to buy Swedish flat-pack furniture.

He was right.

The sat nav took him through Birstall, but promptly out again into the slip of surviving countryside to the north of the grotty little town — then off the road into the long, sweeping driveway of a five-star hotel and spa that Aled recognised from more than one work conference over the years.

"Ta-da!" Gabriel said. "We have a spa afternoon, then dinner this evening and a hotel room for the night."

"We're staying the *night*?"

"Yup!"

Aled groaned, yet parked up anyway. "You're a nightmare."

"I'm a dream come true. *You're* the nightmare right now. So let's unwind in the spa, be civilised over dinner, and then very *un*civilised in our hotel room tonight. Deal?"

Aled laughed. "Deal."

He'd never actually used the spa facilities at the hotel. The last thing he wanted to do was see any of his colleagues in a state of undress in the steam room. But he had to admit that a massage and a soak sounded good right about now.

"Where did you even learn about this place?" he asked as they checked in. He had a suspicion, but it had been a while since Gabriel had had a plaything who'd flashed his cash. "I wouldn't have thought it was Kevin's style."

"It's not," Gabriel said, giving the clearly gay receptionist a flirty smile as they were issued a key card and a handful of leaflets. "Doubt he knows it exists."

"Uh-huh. So who brought you here?"

Gabriel just smirked. Aled followed him to their room, then pinned him up against the door before he could open it.

"Ah-ah," he said. "Tell me."

"If you *must* know —"

"I must."

"Greg."

"*Greg*?"

"Hey, he's into his spa treatments!"

"Are you serious? He fucks in portable toilets."

"And he's very serious about keeping his muscles healthy," Gabriel said, laughing. "It was months and months ago. Remember the Manchester gig and we stayed overnight?"

"Last year? Vaguely."

"Well, we stayed here. Not in Manchester."

"Christ," Aled said, letting go and letting Gabriel open the door. "What did you let him do in exchange for this?"

The hotel room was nothing exceptional — not by Aled's five-star standards, anyway — but the minibar was plentiful and the bed a massive expanse of white in the middle of a generous room. Aled rapped the footboard and asked if Gabriel had brought their toys.

"Nope. You'll have to get inventive."

"Well, I managed at the conference…"

Gabriel grinned, but said nothing. He hefted the case up onto the little sofa tucked into the corner and unzipped it. Aled caught the trunks thrown at his head.

"What have you actually booked me in for?"

"Us!"

"Us, then."

"Two treatments of your choice, an hour and a half in the spa facilities, and then dinner. Thought I did pick your treatments already."

"Which are?"

"Hot stone massage and a foot spa."

It *did* sound nice, but—

"And where are you going to be?"

"Next to you," Gabriel said cheerfully. "I've told you, I've been before."

"And they're all right, are they?"

About *what* hung unspoken between them, but then it was dashed away like a cobweb when Gabriel chuckled.

"Yes. Promise." He looped his arms around Aled's neck and kissed him briefly. "Get into your trunks and let me prove I'm right."

He *was* right. Aled liked the hydrotherapy pool at the gym, but the spa pool was a whole other level. The tension and stress of the last few weeks arranging the move leeched away in the hot water, and the masseuse took care of the rest of it with a blissful hot stone massage. Aled hadn't bothered much with spas since his divorce, but the heat pressing the strain out of his back and Gabriel's fingers hooking gently around his own in the space between their beds was *heaven*.

Suddenly, Aled's idea of a game to take their minds off tomorrow wasn't all that appealing.

Why not be vanilla for the night? Why not be a little romantic?

They floated back to the pool, and Aled didn't let go of Gabriel's hand. To hell with what anyone else thought. He was moving to be near his family, with the best man in his life in the passenger seat. Who gave a shit if Linda from Halifax couldn't make heads or tails of Gabriel's bikini body and scruffy jaw?

He could have taken or left the foot massage — though it turned Gabriel into a puddle of bliss in the next chair — but the last twenty minutes in the water blended the two treatments together until his entire body felt refreshed. He wasn't a chubby middle-aged bloke with greying hair. He was a *god*. And he was having an expensive dinner and a luxury hotel room with a man whose face — never mind the rest of him — could have launched a thousand ships.

The bliss lasted well beyond their treatment session. Aled even got vanilla-handsy on the way back up to their hotel room, and debated between persuading Gabriel to skip out on dinner for a bit of gentle lovemaking in the middle of the cavernous bed, or showing him off to a restaurant full of jealous patrons. In the end, he opted for the showing off — especially when Gabriel wriggled into a pair of slacks that were anything but loose. Aled planted a hand on that perfect bum on the way down in the lift, and didn't bother removing it again until they were shown to their table.

The restaurant was full but surprisingly quiet, and if they attracted a couple of glances from the other customers, the staff didn't bat an eyelash. For once, Aled felt quite comfortable holding hands on the tabletop, and appreciated the plainly romantic candle. A sentimental sensation bubbled up in his chest. The end of their lives in Yorkshire.

And yet brand-new lives beckoned in Cornwall. With Aled's family, Gabriel's boyfriend and a whole new host of opportunities.

"This feels like starting over," he said.

"What?"

"The move," he clarified. "It feels like we're starting again, somehow."

Gabriel smiled, squeezing his hand.

"Can't think of anyone better to start again *with*," Aled continued.

"Are you angling for that vanilla sex you wanted earlier?"

"Mm, maybe. But it's true, too. I'm glad you were on board."

"Well, likewise."

"Me? On board with what?"

"With Chris coming with us," Gabriel said. "And Kevin's visiting schedule."

"'Course."

It had been second nature to agree, in a way. Aled had never been the jealous type, and if he'd never really gone looking for polygamous partners, he also couldn't claim it had been much of an adjustment on his part. So what if their relationship wasn't like everybody else's? So what if their starting over — or their happy ending, depending how he chose to view it — wasn't what other people would want?

"I meant what I said at Suze's wedding."

Gabriel cocked his head.

"If we were the marrying kind, I would."

A faint smile played over Gabriel's lips, and his foot rubbed up against Aled's ankle under the table.

"Me too," he said.

The faux wine arrived. Aled didn't even bother to test it, dismissing the waiter with a wave of his hand and cracking open the bottle on his own, turning the label at Gabriel's frown to show him the proof of its non-alcoholic nature.

"That stuff is revolting."

"I'll order you something else in a minute. Just toast with me."

"To what?"

Aled didn't answer until he'd poured out generous helpings into both glasses, then raised his own.

"To you and me and the people who love us, and to everything that comes next."

"That's a long toast."

"Fine. To happy endings."

Gabriel laughed and clinked his glass against Aled's.

"To the beginning," he countered.

Chapter Twenty-Three

The moving van arrived first thing in the morning.

Gabriel had learned from last time they'd moved house — Aled was best avoided. He'd been up at six, insisting on checking out of the hotel and getting back to the house before Gabriel was even properly awake. And he flapped like nobody's business when it came to having tradesmen and labourers around at the best of times, so Gabriel made the last round of tea, packed the kettle and waited in the car with his phone.

Last time had felt like getting shot of a house that had never really been *his*. Aled's ex-wife's fingerprints had been all over the interior design and décor, and Gabriel had been excited to move into a house where he could leave his own prints. But this time, the excitement was tempered by a thin layer of anxiety. Not as bad as he'd feared — nowhere *near* as bad as he'd been when they'd first moved in together — but anxiety all the same.

After all, this wasn't moving a couple of miles down the road. It was moving a couple of *hundred* miles down the motorway.

Still, he let Aled boss everyone around and stayed out of the way. Only when the movers slammed the doors on the last box did Gabriel slide out of the car and go for one last walk-through of a house he'd never see again.

The empty rooms gaped. Shadows on the paint betrayed the former locations of their photos. Aled was running the vacuum cleaner over the dust bunnies that had bred under their furniture. Had the mantelpiece always been that large?

"All right?" Aled asked as he switched the vacuum cleaner off.

"Yeah. Just looks a little strange."

Aled hummed. The removal guy came back in for him to sign some papers, but once he'd gone and the van had roared off down the street, Aled held up his arms. Gabriel stepped into the hug, burrowing for a moment.

"Sure you're okay?" Aled murmured.

"Yeah. It's just a little weird."

"I can always drop you off at Kevin's and get you a train ticket if —"

"No," Gabriel said. "He's already bought my tickets for my first visit. And I want to see everything go in the new house."

He'd still only seen pictures. Kevin had called him crazy for not going to see it, but Gabriel didn't care. A house was a house. He trusted Chris' and Aled's judgement, and if it didn't fit after a couple of years, they could move again. It wasn't like Gabriel wasn't used to changing his living arrangements by now.

Most importantly, the new house was right next to Chris.

"Come on," he said, wriggling out of the hug. "Let's get on the road. Need to get there before they do."

Aled snorted. "And you've been riding shotgun in my car for *how* long?"

"Good point."

The car was packed with their valuables, the usual snacks for the long drive south, and a box full of their sex toys. Aled had been a bit funny about putting it in the van, as if the movers would have a rummage. Like the guys *wouldn't* have figured out they were hefting a gay couple's shit around.

They wedged the vacuum cleaner on top of the bags in the boot, slammed it, and…that was that.

Me: Bye bye Yorkshire :(

Gabriel fired off the text as Aled shifted into first gear and pulled out, for the last time, from his usual parking spot. The village trundled away behind them as he headed for the motorway, and Kevin's reply came through, appropriately enough, just as they reached the slip road.

Kevin: Until the seventeenth x

Me: Yeah :)

Kevin: Remember your rules

Me: Yep

"Kevin?"

"Yeah."

"Everything all right?"

"Yep," Gabriel said. "Being told to remember my rules."

Stay in touch.

That was the rule. There weren't many rules outside of their games. In fact, only three. And the biggest one was that.

Stay in touch.

It might be Cornwall. It might be hundreds of miles. But he had to touch base every single day, or Kevin would drive that battered old Sprinter van of his all the way down to St Ives to find out why he hadn't. And in four weeks, Gabriel would get on the train and come back. Dinner with Judith and the kids again. Maybe the night in the workshop at the bottom of the garden, or maybe in the spare room.

Their door was always going to be open for him.

Aled put his foot down in the fast lane, and Yorkshire shot past in a blur of green and grey. The radio sputtered and died at Nottingham before jumping onto a local station past Leicester, and Birmingham was a grey smudge at the edges of Gabriel's vision as they cruised around the south of the city towards the M5.

"You'll get another speeding ticket."

"Meh."

The M5 itself was a boring stretch of traffic jams and nothingness, and Gabriel must have dozed off, because Bristol wasn't *that* close to Birmingham. They stopped at the services — Aled was like clockwork, and always needed a leak around that point in the journey — and Gabriel ventured out under brooding storm clouds to get some hot food. Waiting in line for some burgers, he fired off a text to Chris.

Me: At Bristol x

Chris: Okay :) I probably won't be in when you get here. Exploring.

Me: That's okay. Probably a good thing. Aled is fussy about moving house.

Chris: Why do you think I went out today??

Gabriel chuckled.

Me: Didn't rescue me though, did you?

Chris: You never asked.

"Not the *point*, Chris..."
"What can I get you, sir?"
He put in a big order, then returned to his texting.

Me: Will you be back tonight?

Chris: Yeah

Me: See you this evening then xxx

He wasn't too surprised Chris had bailed on their arrival. He probably suspected exactly what Gabriel suspected—that Tom and Suze would want to come and welcome Aled to the neighbourhood. And Chris was going to need a few more controlled meetings with them before he got entirely comfortable.

He made it back to the car with the burgers before the heavens opened, and made a start on his while half-listening to the radio and the rain on the roof. Aled had to sprint back through the downpour, and sat steaming in the driver's seat for a few minutes with his own junk food.

"Decide to get this in before we met up with Chris?"

"Yep!"

Aled chuckled. "Break into the biscuits, too, then. He'll confiscate them."

"He can *try*."

They did break into the tin, though, before binning the telltale wrappers and setting off again. Rain cleaned the windscreen at Weston-Super-Mare, and the sun returned at Exeter before they leapt off the motorway and plunged into Devon. The wide, spacious roads gave way to a familiar battle through back lanes to avoid the traffic, and they burst out just shy of St Ives, buried in Cornish fields, overeager songbirds and a strangely wealthy countryside.

Gabriel had lived in a lot of places, but never the country.

Aled turned away at the edge of St Ives and headed back out into the fields. Gabriel sat up and stared at every passing gate. Was this it? This? How about this one? And finally, just before the road narrowed into a single track, Aled eased off through a wide, open gate and up a shared drive before turning off through another gate and rolling the car into a gravelled driveway bordered by grassy lawn and there, cupping a circle of yard space, sat two bungalows that Gabriel recognised from hours memorising their adverts.

"Here we are."

The van hadn't arrived yet—probably not surprisingly—but a familiar car was parked outside the new house. As Aled needlessly parallel-parked in front of Tom's car, the driver's door opened and Tom himself stepped out, waving.

"Hey," Gabriel called, winding the window down. "Have you come to help?"

"Yep."

"Good. I'll stay here then."

"Lazy shit," Aled complained.

Gabriel sniped back before getting out. He took the keys and marched off for the door. Let them call the moving guys and get estimated arrival times and all that shit. Gabriel was going to finally get a look at the place—and find Chris, if he was around.

The front door opened straight into a large, open living area. The photos had been accurate. The empty space invited a multitude of options, and Gabriel explored each end of the rectangular house to find a roomy kitchen, a neat and brand-new bathroom and a spare room that was surprisingly generous. Spiral stairs wound upwards into the roof space, where the master bedroom nestled under the eaves, and an odd little pantry turned out to be the cellar stairs. An inviting den yawned under the house, stretching out until Gabriel was sure the second set had to lead up into Chris' house. He tried the door at the top of them, but was disappointed to find Chris had either locked it or barricaded it from the other side. Still, it offered some intriguing possibilities for breaking-and-entering games once they'd settled in.

He retreated back into the house, already making plans in his head. The bungalow itself was smaller than their old cottage—but there was plenty of room. They could have a conservatory built on one side of the house. The cellar would make a great playroom. A shared summerhouse could box off a third side of the yard.

This could work.

This could *really* work.

Aled and Tom were gossiping at the front door, and Gabriel dropped down from the bottom step to wedge himself under Aled's arm.

"At the risk of scaring the vanilla guest," he said, "the cellar can be our playroom."

"The play—nope, never mind," Tom said hastily.

"Like it?" Aled asked.

"Yep."

"Just as well," he said. "I was hoping to persuade you into that."

"Done and done," Gabriel said. "Where's the van?"

"Just passed Exeter."

"And Chris?"

"Didn't answer. Left him a voicemail. I think he mentioned something about a bike club, though."

"Dinner first, then?" Gabriel suggested. "We could raid a chippie or something and eat it on the floor."

"Deal. Tom, go get food."

Tom grumbled, but was dismissed effectively enough. Aled started hefting in the boxes from the car. Gabriel started to unpack their overnight bags. Afternoon turned into evening. More food came and went. Gabriel tucked himself out of the way again once the van arrived, only venturing out to collect his bike and stash it in the cellar. He wasn't too keen on having workmen around at the best of times, and workmen going through his stuff was definitely no better.

When the house fell quiet, though, he emerged from the cellar and ventured back into the house. Their furniture looked out of place on the hardwood floors, absent carpets and their usual cushions and throws. Stacks of boxes had been turned into towers. The bed had been abandoned in the middle of the bedroom rather than put in a proper place, and the spare bed had been abandoned in the living room.

But their cuddle chair was in the perfect place, tucked into the corner, angled to stare out over the garden on rainy days, and Aled had already found its blankets.

"Hey!" Gabriel called.

Aled's reply came from upstairs. "What?"

"Where's Tom?"

"Gone to get Euan from his nan's house."

"Is he coming back?"

"Him and Suze will probably come round, yeah. Depends if they can get Euan to sleep and strong-arm Tom's sister into babysitting." Footsteps creaked. Aled leaned over the banisters to frown at Gabriel. "Why?"

"Cuddle chair's ready."

Aled chuckled. "You want a nap?"

Gabriel nodded. "Yeah. Before the chaos starts again. It'll feel like home, then."

Well, it would be a start.

Chapter Twenty-Four

It was dark when Chris coasted the bike up the tiny private road to the gate.

The gate itself had been shut, and only Aled's car gleamed under the moonlit sky. Chris let out a breath. Good. He could put off more socialising for another day. He was all peopled out.

He'd spent the morning unpacking his gear, and the afternoon exploring St Ives. He'd not really wanted to be in the way when Aled's family came to greet him and help him move in, and he ought to get started on settling into this new world anyway. Once he'd found posters for a cycling club, he'd decided to grit his teeth and go make some friends. If he did that, he didn't have to feel awkward about avoiding Aled's friends.

And it had worked.

The guy who ran the club was a nice bloke. Chris had managed to get into an easy conversation with a couple of the other regulars, who'd pointed him in the direction of a trustworthy bike shop in the town. And the route had been a gentle climb along the coast, challenging enough to keep him interested but easy enough that he didn't feel out of his depth and unfit in front of a gaggle of strangers. He'd even stayed for a drink with Ian, the organiser, and a couple in their fifties called Harry and Ann who wanted to pump him for knowledge on the best routes in Somerset.

So by the time he got back to the house — back *home* — it was well after dark, and a chilly fog was beginning to settle over the hedges and trees.

The moving van had left furrows in the gravel, and the lights were on in the bungalow opposite his own. Chris smuggled his bike past their windows and let himself in, hurriedly changing in the dark of his new bedroom before testing out his theory.

They weren't the type to lock their playroom door.

Chris had locked his, more out of a security habit than any real intention to keep either of them out. He eased the bolt back and sneaked downstairs, fumbling for the light switch in the dark for a moment. The lights were boring halogen bulbs dangling from the ceiling, and he made a mental note to swap out the fittings to allow for something nicer.

The cellar itself was still empty, save for Gabriel's bike propped up against the wall, and Chris tiptoed to the second set of stairs and inched up them, testing for creaks. Sure enough, their pantry door was unlocked, and he slipped out into the kitchen that — so far — was identical to his own. Except for the pizza boxes on the counter and several empty soft-drink cans. He rolled his eyes at the *Aled-ness* of it all and opened the door.

"Chris!"

Gabriel leapt up out of the cuddle chair and slammed into him full-force. Chris grinned, hugging back. Aled just waved a lazy hand and turned his attention back to the TV. Like Chris was always supposed to just appear in their house like that. The feeling made Chris warm from the inside out.

"Is it safe to visit?" he asked anyway.

"Coast is clear," Gabriel said cheerfully. "Though we're under orders. Next Saturday, all three of us, pub lunch with Tom and Suze and Euan and Pumpkin."

"Pumpkin?"

"That's what Suze is calling her baby bump," Aled called from the chair. "The sonographer couldn't tell if it was a boy or a girl at last week's scan, so they're calling it Pumpkin while they argue over names."

"Ew."

"You're telling me…"

"I still say Maggie is a nice name," Gabriel sniffed.

"It's awful," Chris said seriously.

"*Thank* you!" Aled called.

"Oh, shut up," Gabriel grumbled, then shook Chris by the collar of his polo shirt and grinned. "Did you go to the cycling club? Was it good? Can I come to the next one? Is—"

"Oi! Trying to watch a film here!"

"Then *pause* it, you fuc—"

"You watch your language."

Gabriel stuck his tongue out. Chris clapped a hand over his mouth.

"Oh no you don't," he said. "I'm not up for one of his games."

Aled laughed. "You can stay. Put that sorry mess in the cellar."

"I don't think so," Chris replied. "My door's unlocked. He'll cause havoc."

"I'll make him a cage at some point."

Gabriel whined, wriggled out of Chris' grip and called them both bastards.

"Whatever. You coming back, or am I resorting to cuddling Chris in this chair instead?"

Chris made a face. Aled laughed and climbed out of the chair, relocating to the sofa. It had been awkwardly dumped in the middle of the room, but Chris figured they'd just wanted to get shot of the removal men. He could sympathise. His own meagre belongings were still a bit haphazard. So he sank onto the opposite side without a murmur about the odd position, and they both expectantly looked to Gabriel to fill the gap between them.

Instead, he folded his arms over his chest.

"Why should I sit there?" he demanded. "You want to stick me in a cage. That's not very nice."

"I'm not a very nice man," Aled countered. "So you can sit down and behave, or Chris will go home and leave you to me."

Gabriel's eyes narrowed. Chris smirked, watching him weigh it up. He probably *did* want a bit of rough fun to break in the new home — but he clearly wanted to enjoy having them both within arm's reach too.

And eventually, the novelty of them both being there won. He sank down into the middle spot with a grumpy huff.

"Did Tom and Suze help you move in?" Chris asked.

"Tom did. Suze had to take Euan for his jabs. But they brought pizza once he was pincushioned, and we got the telly hooked up. Most important part," Aled said. "What about you? Have you settled in yet?"

"Eh. Some of it. I don't have as much stuff as you, though. And I could do with a hand getting my mattress upstairs if you don't mind."

"In the morning?"

"Sure."

It was relaxed and easy, like it had been towards the end of Gabriel's recovery in Yorkshire. Chris sagged back into the cushions and tried to catch up with the film. One of the *Transformers* ones, but hell if he knew which. Gabriel offered a cup of tea. Aled asked after Chris' job-hunting success.

It was like he ought to be here.

When Gabriel came back from the kitchen, he sat in Chris' lap and slung his feet over Aled's. The warm weight was more than a little bit nice, and Chris buried his nose in Gabriel's hair and breathed in the familiar smell in the unfamiliar room. Where would Gabriel sleep tonight? Would he give warning or just turn up? Would they all hold keys to every door on the plot, or would only Gabriel have that privilege?

There was so much left to work out, yet —

Yet Chris didn't particularly want to bother. Not tonight. Let tonight just be about the bad film on the TV, cold cans of stomach-rotting filth from the fridge, and Gabriel's questions about the bike club and whether St Ives was big enough to have a yoga class he could go to and help his damaged leg now he was well out of reach of his old physiotherapist.

They could sort registering with GPs, copying keys, finding driving instructors for Chris, and everything else in the morning.

Right now...

Right now, Gabriel was in his lap, Aled was running a sardonic commentary, and Chris was trying to persuade them to switch over to *Airplane!*, in which the long-dead Leslie Nielsen was alive and well in a disaster spoof that made Chris never want to board a plane again as long as he lived.

Everything else could wait.

Right here, right now, all was well.

Chapter Twenty-Five

The following Saturday, Tom texted the details of a decent pub just down the coast, and reported that they did a mean fish and thick-cut chips.

Aled, all alone in the house, forwarded the text to his boyfriend's health nut of a partner and finished hanging the sheets out to dry before going inside to get changed.

It was already starting to feel like home.

He'd started work on Wednesday. Chris had taken up an apprenticeship in the kitchens of Tom's St Ives hotel and was working on an application to the local police force. And Gabriel would be donning a suit and tie next month when a woman at Suze's office went on maternity leave. The work had been found, and the budgets shuffled until they were back in the black. Life was starting to settle once more.

But more than that, the bungalows felt like *theirs*.

Chris had already planted some cherry trees by the gate and started turning the earth for a vegetable garden on his side of the drive. Aled had spent the morning laying borders so Gabriel could resurrect his love of flowers from their little garden in Newmillardam. The curtains were up in the windows, the rugs were down on the bedroom floor and the first post had arrived through the door that very morning.

They lived here now.

Sure, Aled was still trying to remember which neighbours were Sam and Jean, and which were Ted and Mary, but he'd get there. Said neighbours had yet to figure out what kind of weird the three blokes up the lane were, but they'd get there too. Bin day seemed to be optional. The council still hadn't cottoned on that they existed, despite several phone calls.

But the weirdest part was driving. He set up the sat nav as he got in the car, still totally at sea when it came to where *anywhere* was in Cornwall just yet. He hadn't even quite memorised the route to Suze's house—not that he was dumb enough to tell her that. And Chris had snidely asked more than once if he knew how to close a gate.

Speaking of gates…

He hopped back out to shut the gate behind him, and by the time he shut the driver's door, his phone had vibrated in his pocket. He paused to swipe it open, and smirked.

Chris: Hey ;) Guess who hasn't changed his passcode?

It was followed by a selfie of Gabriel, looking windswept and thoroughly fuckable, flashing a peace sign by the sea. Clifftops, going by the distance.

Chris: We're just turning around to head for the pub. See you there! Xxx

Me: What have you stopped for? Tired already?

Chris: We're at Shagging-On-Sea, obviously!!

Chris: Oops, caught.

Aled waited, grinning. And sure enough, eventually —

Chris: I'm coming to the pub. Just threw Gabriel off a cliff.

Me: You're not supposed to put that sort of thing in text messages.

Me: Police'll find it.

Me: Now we're both busted.

Chris: Shit, yeah. Fine. I'll go fetch him and dust him off.

Me: Good idea. See you soon.

He tossed the phone back on the passenger seat, checked the sat nav once more and set off.

The Cornish countryside was basking under a hot sun, and he drove with the windows down. Farm traffic and tourists competed on the narrow excuse for a main road, and Aled cruised along behind an overloaded people carrier without a care in the world, drumming his fingers absently on the steering wheel in time to a tune on the radio. He didn't even *like* R'n'B.

The pub was just off the so-called main road, visible but protected by a large hedge. Aled snagged the last parking spot and, as he had no texts, headed into the blissfully quiet bar for some shelter. The biggest downside to Cornwall so far was the heat compared to West Yorkshire. He was going to need to up his game with the sun cream.

With Chris and Gabriel a few miles out yet, Aled took advantage and had a quick cider, crisp and cold from the cellar. He headed out to claim a shady spot and wait, keeping an eye on his phone so he knew to either down the cider or toss it into the nearest plant before Gabriel arrived. But thankfully, they were in no rush either. Tom and Suze arrived with Euan and the as-yet-unnamed baby bump first, and a second round of drinks came in before two bikes shot past the hedgerows and the squeak of brakes sounded on the corner.

"Here they come," Aled said, and hastily dumped the empty cider glass on a nearby picnic bench.

They arrived dusty from the dry summer, Gabriel stooping for a quick kiss and Aled turning his face aside only just in time.

"Cider," he said by way of explanation, and got to his feet. "Let me."

"Deal. My legs are *killing* me."

Food orders flew. Aled was sent back off to the pub with a menu, a list and a bundle of cash. By the time he came back, his shady spot had been claimed by the equally fair Chris, and a sun patch left for him opposite Gabriel and next to a squalling Euan. The baby was fussed and passed around while his father ran off into the pub to reheat some paste, and Aled revelled in the noisy, messy, crowded chaos.

There, holding a screaming infant he couldn't stand, it struck home.

Home.

He was home.

And as they settled — baby pacified, drinks flowing, food arriving — the feeling didn't subside. Gabriel's feet were between Aled's under the bench while he cosied up to Chris for a kiss, stealing food off his plate while Chris was suitably distracted. Euan was enthusiastically spreading his own food all over his face while Tom attempted to feed him in a dignified manner, and Suze sat back with her lemonade and laughed at the futility of the attempt, one hand resting on her prominent baby bump. Aled batted a wasp away from his ear and smiled, even as the sun singed his ears and a burst of pain said the little bastard had stung him.

It was a long way from Yorkshire and ex-wives, scattered ashes and thankless jobs.

His job was never going to change the world. Mum and Dad and Nan weren't coming back. The household budget might never really recover. There'd be more sleepless nights and anxiety-induced safewords.

But in the blazing sun, the bench populated by every living person that he loved, Aled couldn't see the cloud on his silver linings. He was heading for forty, and he'd started his life over again in a lonely midlife crisis — yet here he was.

Sitting in the midst of his happy ending, with a whole new beginning.

Want to see more from this author? Here's a taster for you to enjoy!

Enough
Matthew J. Metzger

Excerpt

He could smell the fire.

He was blind. His eyes streamed. The curling wallpaper crackled and hissed. His skin was burning. The air in his lungs seared him from the inside out. And there was nowhere to go — no escape from the heat, no escape from the orange towers and acrid black smoke, no *air*.

"Ezra!"

The smoke wrapped itself around his teeth and tongue like a grotesque mockery of a kiss, and there was no reply but the roar of hot air and climbing fire. The house was burning. *The house was burning!*

"Ezra! Ez!"

A scream. A piercing scream, like nothing he'd ever heard, but before he could move, the wooden boards crumbled to ash and he was falling, tearing through the shreds of stairs into the inferno, and —

Jesse hit the carpet with a thump and jarred himself awake.

The flat was quiet. The streetlight touched the other side of the curtains with a faint orange light. There was no smoke, no fire, no sound. Nothing.

Jesse dragged himself back onto the bed. The sheets were impossibly tangled and his tank top stuck to him with sweat. His wrist ached in its brace where he'd bumped it, but the panic hadn't quite eased its grip on his heart or his lungs, and he fumbled for his phone, ignoring the pain.

Thank God for speed dial.

The clock on the side said two-fifty-eight, and the phone rang six times before the line coughed and crackled and a sleepy voice, tinged in the early hours with the fading edges of a Welsh accent, mumbled a vague sort of question.

"Ez?"

There was a rustle of sheets. "Jesse?"

"Oh, God," Jesse breathed. The air escaped in a rush, loud and hard. His lungs shook with the effort. "Shit. I just— I needed to check—"

"Jess? What's happened, sweetheart?"

The soft roll of his vowels, the accent entirely muted when he was properly awake, was as comforting as a hug, and Jesse coughed out, "Nightmare," before thinking twice. Ezra was okay. He was okay. It was all okay.

"Oh, sweetheart," Ezra murmured, low and crooning. "Do you want to tell me about it?"

"I need—can I come over? I know it's late and I know you have work in the morning, but—I just—I need—"

"No," Ezra interrupted, and Jesse's stomach twisted violently.

"*Please*, Ez, I—"

"Hey, hey, hey." Ezra cut him off. "Hey, stop, calm down, sweetheart. I *meant* you can't come here. You don't sound okay, not to me, and I don't want you to go out like this, so I'll come to you, all right?"

Jesse exhaled, the twist easing. "Okay."

"You okay if I hang up, or do you want me to put the phone on speaker?"

"Can—speaker," Jesse swallowed against the nausea. He was still shaking, he realised faintly. "I just—I couldn't find you, Ez. The house was burning and I couldn't find you, and I—I need to hear you. You don't have to talk to me, but I need to hear you."

"Okay." The phone crackled again and clunked, and suddenly Ezra's voice was loud and echoing. Soothing. The Welsh hint was fading, and Jesse could suddenly hear him dressing, but he was *there*. "Was it my house or the one last week?"

"Yours," Jesse said. "I was on the stairs, and they gave way, and I woke up. I couldn't find you."

"If my house was on fire, I would probably be in the kitchen having caused it," Ezra said, and yawned loudly. "Make yourself useful, sweetheart, and make up a brew for me? I've not slept long."

Jesse knew better than to apologise. He shrugged out of his sweat-soaked pyjamas and pulled on a pair of jogging bottoms before taking the phone through the narrow hall into the kitchen. The kitchen window overlooked the main road. A police car trailed idly by on the prowl. Phone to his ear, he listened to Ezra swear sleepily at his cupboard, and the soft sounds of those narrow feet padding downstairs.

"Sweetheart?"

"Mm?" Jesse listened to the front door and the heavy sound of the key.

"I'm going to hang up while I drive. You all right for ten minutes until I get there?"

"Yeah," Jesse croaked. His heart had come down out of the rafters, and he could breathe. The streetlights didn't look threatening anymore. He just felt…shaky. Sick and shaky and scared. "Yeah, Ez, I'll be fine."

"Okay. Love you."

The dial tone was immediate. Jesse dropped the phone to the counter and switched on the kettle, staring out of the window and waiting, arms folded against the chill. It wasn't the first nightmare, and it wouldn't be the last. He usually managed one a week without fail, and the injury hadn't helped matters. But they didn't usually involve Ezra in burning buildings. They didn't usually involve losing him.

And Jesse couldn't stomach the thought of losing him.

Which was a bit scary in itself. They'd only met eight months ago. At a gay bar, of all places — the one place where he went to meet sex partners, not partner partners. Jesse had thought the freckled blond with the dark eyes was pretty in the neon lights and had bought him a drink, talked him into a dance, bought him another. Kissed him at the back of the dance floor — and had promptly found himself alone, but with a phone number in his back pocket.

He'd wanted sex. That was all he'd been after. Sex with a pretty guy. But then they'd gone on a date and he'd met Ezra properly, and he was lost. Ezra wasn't just a handsome face and nice legs. Ezra was the world. He was Jesse's world, and it had only been eight months, but Jesse still knew that this was it, for him. Ezra was it. There would never be anyone else like him.

So he stood in a tense vigil at the window, waiting for the faithful little Peugeot 207 to creep around the corner. Waiting for Ezra to come, because there was emotional shock and there was sense, and the two weren't in line right now. He knew Ezra was okay. He knew it. He'd answered the phone. He'd been sleepy and understanding and sworn at his cupboard. He was fine.

But Jesse still needed to reach out and touch him, just to make sure. *Somehow.*

The little blue car was lonely on the three-in-the-morning road, and Jesse propped the door of his flat to creep down the communal stairs and open the main door. Ezra had gotten sort-of dressed, in jeans and an open check shirt, feet shoved into his trainers without socks, and his hair was wild and fluffy, in gleeful disarray, as he locked the car and wrapped himself around Jesse in a tight, warm hug.

Jesse clung back until something creaked, and pressed the side of his face against that wild hair.

"You're all right, sweetheart," Ezra murmured.

Jesse squeezed again until Ezra's grip on the nape of his neck tightened in warning, then he let go and dragged Ezra up the silent stairs by the hand. Concrete stairs. They wouldn't collapse in a fire until the whole building came down.

He didn't say a word until he'd pressed the requested tea into Ezra's hands, locked the door again and bundled them both back to the messy bed. Ezra was equally silent, taking a couple of mouthfuls before abandoning the tea, stripping to his underwear and crawling into the mess to mould himself into Jesse's arms.

"There you go," he murmured lowly, kissing Jesse's encroaching stubble and stroking a hand gently through his hair. "Feel better now?"

"Mm," Jesse pressed his nose into Ezra's neck, tangling their legs together. He could feel a strong pulse in Ezra's jugular. He could feel the rough skin of the bumpy scar on Ezra's shoulder under his fingertips. He could feel the fuzzy mess of Ezra's hair, usually styled and stiff in that messy-but-it's-on-purpose-so-it's-okay manner, now just loose and wild. He could feel *him*. "Thank you."

"Thank me again tomorrow afternoon when I'm grumpy and exhausted after two hours of the Year Nines."

"Okay," Jesse agreed, sliding his arms completely around Ezra's back until he enveloped him. They didn't often sleep cuddled together—or even together at all, between Ezra's eight-to-four and Jesse's shifts—but he needed this. He *needed* it.

"Mind if I go to sleep?"

"No," Jesse squirmed until Ezra got the hint and tucked his head under his chin. His hair tickled. Jesse kissed the top of his head and wished he had the easy grace with language that Ezra did. Wished he could express himself properly. Wished he could talk as easily as he hugged. But all that came out was, "I just needed to touch you."

Ezra said nothing to that, simply shifting until he was comfortable, one arm over Jesse's ribs and the other tucked over his own waist in a casual sort of drop. Ezra was *long*—long limbs, long neck, all willowy lines and bendy joints, and he settled like water into the bulkier, stiffer contours of Jesse's body.

But he fit, and he fit perfectly, and Jesse wrapped him up and held him, breathing in the smell of store-brand shampoo and cheap aftershave until the last traces of the nightmare-induced fear washed away.

It was still a long time before he slept.

PUBLISHING

Sign up for our newsletter and find out about all our
romance book releases, eBook sales and promotions,
sneak peeks and FREE romance books!

About the Author

Matthew J. Metzger is an asexual, transgender British author juggling books, an office job and a love of travel with the human need for sleep once in a while. He writes both adult and young adult books focusing on LGBT+ characters and their relationships, particularly those from the less salubrious areas in which he was dragged up over the years.

On the very rare occasions that Matt isn't writing, he can usually be found at the gym, halfway up a mountain or collecting new tattoos. (And yes, he does have book ink...)

Matthew loves to hear from readers. You can find his contact information, website details and author profile page at https://www.pride-publishing.com